with best wishes!

— Bill Jordan

Beccles
'96

NUMBER RANK AND NAME

Bill Jardine

FINE PUBLISHING
Toft Monks, Beccles
Suffolk

'The first quality of a soldier is fortitude in enduring fatigue and hardship; bravery but the second. Poverty, hardship and misery are the school of a good soldier'

Napoleon

First published UK in 1990 by
Fine Publishing
Priory Lane
Toft Monks, Beccles
Suffolk

ISBN 1 873248 00 8

Printed and bound by
Creasey Flood Ltd
Tower Road, Pakefield
Lowestoft, Suffolk

FOREWORD

by

Brigadier H. J. Hickman CBE

Honorary Colonel Commandant Royal Pioneers

Successful writing of any military history or comment on war relies heavily on stories of individuals' experiences if a truly authentic feel is to be part of the result. The more personal and familiar the tale, the greater the feeling of authenticity. It is from these storytellers and gifted observers of the small-scale human interest scenes of soldiers everyday life in war that we obtain the detail which is otherwise too soon forgotten and lost. Such detail, presented in truly kaleidoscopic mixture, is the stuff of *Number Rank and Name*.

This collection of stories pretends no historical pedigree. Its value is in the authentic ring which emerges from every page.

Everyone who served in the Forties and Fifties will revel in the familiarity of the scenes described and recognise the characters – or someone who would double for them. It happens that the author was a Sapper and Pioneer but, in truth, these tales need no cap badge. They could have come from all corners of the Army and many Royal Navy and Royal Air Force ones too. Doesn't everyone who lived in a Nissen in Winter have a coalyard story to tell?

The characters and qualities of the personalities; the apparent idiocies of the machinery of a huge army; the fortitude of those closest to the action, frustrations and difficulties; the welter of colour and memory; it is all here. In a highly staccato style not unlike those war-time telegrams the author has captured it all.

Bill Jardine has done something else not easily achieved, for these stories are often easier told than written.. He has made the collection hugely enjoyable, retained the truth, and yet produced an enduring snapshot of the British character at war. Here is a book to be devoured or dipped into with equal certainty of finding something familiar, to ponder about if you were not there, and to chuckle over, whoever you are. We should all be glad he has written it down for us.

PREFACE

These pages will offer little to satisfy the reading habits of those who thrill to the misguided 'glamour' of war.

Striving, albeit unsuccessfully, to strictly limit the wretched personal pronoun, one's aim has been to reflect something of the very ordinary individual's impressions of life in uniform.

Most Second World War service people, now veterans, are mighty glad to have 'done their bit' – whatever, wherever, and for however long.

In all arms of the Forces logistics are vital. Like myself a considerable number of contemporaries served with Supply and Support Troops in the advance from Normandy into Germany on which most of these selected cameos are based. Many will tell me there's more missing from this lot than a dog has fleas!

The thoughts of my generation now go out to our successors – the modern Serviceman and Servicewoman presently serving in an increasingly difficult, uncertain, and fast changing world. And to their loved ones.

For his Foreword I am grateful to, and thank, Brigadier John Hickman CBE, recently retired Director of my own Corps: himself at one time a Private soldier. I would also like to thank Major Colin Spears, present Corps Secretary of The Royal Pioneers for his kind encouragement.

DEDICATION

In Comradeship, remembering all having worn Service uniform . . . and those still doing so . . . destined to remain hidden in some Nominal Roll, maybe at a distant time to be discovered in dusty archives as 'just another' Number Rank and Name.

B.J.
Beccles
Suffolk

CONTENTS

Miscellaneous

Last on Parade

From a Lanark Primary Training Centre, permanent staff bristling with Argyle & Sutherland Highlanders, Black Watch, Cameronians, KOSB's, Scots Guards and other equally famous Scots Regiments, this Private posted to Royal Engineers, Longmoor in Hampshire, overnight became a Sapper.

At Weavers Down Camp, occupied by Movement Control Technical Training & Depot Battalion, new arrivals exchanged pleasantries.

Four struck up an immediate rapport.

How naturally it happened!

Within hours, great pals!

On the morrow, chivvying each other along, determined to be punctual and make a good start, we prepared for the first Morning Parade.

Ten minutes to zero hour yours truly was taken short!

Three mates insisted on waiting.

Fortunately, with a full minute to spare, other comrades were being joined on the parade ground.

A Sergeant's voice ripped out.

'Hi! You four! You're bloody late! Stand over there!'

Consulting wristwatches, four heads shook in disbelief. Which was manna to Sergeant Hanson! Casting doubts on parentage and promising life impotency for daring to challenge authority, our isolation didn't satisfy him.

Histrionically, we were brought to attention, right dress, eyes front, left turn, quick march (in the direction from whence we'd come), halt, followed by every possible drill sequence until, facing inwards, we were standing at ease.

All of which made it considerably later before the customary time for the RSM to be called upon to take over the proceedings.

Parade dismissed, it was not a very amused quartet which found itself the nucleus of Depot Fatigue Party and allotted the least attractive of all tasks!

Sitting on an upturned beer crate at the back of the Sergeant's Mess, facing at least a dozen buckets full of potatoes, my instructions had been to peel the lot, thereafter stand to attention and await the next order.

Applying myself to those equally miserable spuds, after the long and hectic initial stint in Scotland how could one think of anything but the relative proximity of home?

Had the chance of getting that anxiously awaited very first short leave been blown?

And so promptly too?

Sergeants came and went. Without a word. Not a glance.

Two hours passed.

Suddenly, a srong, resonant, voice from behind.

Unmistakeably the RSM's.

Jumping to attention, I was looking into a friendly face.

'Live somewhere in the London area, Sapper?' he asked.

'Correct Sir'.

'Married?'

'Sir'.

'Children?'

'One, Sir'.

'If you hurry you'll catch the 10.45 train. Pick up a 48-hours pass at Depot Office!'

Stunned, I stuttered my thanks.

'No, lad!' he cut me short 'Don't thank ME! Thank Sergeant Hanson!'

With a wry smile he strode off.

I caught that train!

O unique Longmoor Military Railway – the lifeline to liberty, on which, after hours of training, one learned to pass a metal ring for clearance, how vividly you are remembered!

But the RSM, so very much more!

A really splendid type. A gentleman. In civil life a train driver.

Eventful months later I sought him out not only to say goodbye but to thank him for his firm discipline – always with fairness and justice.

With characteristic modesty he waived this aside. Just a nod of appreciation, and whilst shaking hands a flash of memory recalling our first meeting.

'Well Sapper' he said 'At least you'll remember we're not ALL cheats here!'

Pity! Something I've always regretted! I never saw him again.

After D-Day, no-one else did either.

One Bucket of Coal

Bitter winter had struck.

Camp plumbing repeatedly froze up.

In the Ablutions Block, toilet flushings had long since ceased.

Concrete floors of nissen huts glistened with ice.

Coal rationing, after a meagre issue for weeks, stopped altogether.

Customary jostling for warmth around the central stove ceased. It stood empty.

The Coal Compound, with its precious depleted stock, had been barricaded by a new fifteen feet high wire-netting fence, menacingly topped with barbed wire. Its gates strengthened, chained and padlocked.

A whole perishing week had made normal use of living huts unbearable. Off-duty hours brought record attendances at NAAFI, which managed some warmth.

The night's kip had to be faced. Fully clothed bodies shivered below frozen blankets, greatcoats atop.

There had been talk of smoke curling up from other huts. This would be checked. Systematic tours, at odd hours, confirmed the talk had substance! Worse still, each night more huts appeared to be enjoying the luxury of a fire, however small!

Since the clampdown on rationing, Hut 21 seemed the only one which had not emitted smoke at some time or other. Hut 21 housed the P.O. Course. Watched men, living on a perpetual knife-edge of uncertainty. Hut 21 status could afford no unguarded moment. One mistake and it was back, with immediate curtains, to 'normal duty'! Aspirations shattered!

The cold spell worsened: temperatures fell to an all-time low.

The Ablutions Cleaner, who was also king of the Coal Compound, had been thoroughly checked out. No way was there the slightest chance of any co-operation from him!

Frequent watches kept on the Coal stock confirmed suspicions. Definite gaps had somehow appeared in the whitewashed perimeter of the heap. After each poaching, re-whitewashing!

On the whole of Longmoor Plain there could not possibly be a more bitter habitation than Hut 21, but the risk of stealing coal couldn't even be thought about. Or could it? Paralysed with cold, frozen, now desperate occupants were somehow secretly canvassed, drawn together and gathered around the empty stove. It was speedily agreed, whatever the consequences, at least one bucketful of coal must be acquired. Tacit no volunteers would be forthcoming two names would be drawn for.

Under eagle-eyed scrutiny, nobody's name missed, slips were written and checked. With even greater watchfulness, these dropped into the coal scuttle. Using the poker, each man would give the lot a ceremonial stir. For the magic of a few hours precious warmth in the hut who would be the two to risk everything? Ritual under way the banter of the blessings and benedictions was much too theatrical; distinctly edgy!

Premonition, E.S.P., call it what you will, I knew one of those names would be mine, and when announced, for ironic reasons known only to me, guffawed out loudly!

Collective responsibility was sworn. Names would not be divulged either under torture or threat of the whole Course being chucked out.

We accepted misfortune. This was destiny at work!

For the required break-in, wild and wonderful ideas were offered and discussed. All had some weakness. An element of detection.

Secret meeting dispersed, the two of us agreed on swift action. Get it over! Why delay matters? Caught in the act, the promised solidarity would be of no value at all. Together we devised strategy. All the 'clever' ploys dismissed. The one and only possibility of success the most difficult – a straight frontal foray over that high fence and barbed wire. And at dead of night. That very night! Method unknown to others!

Guardroom procedures mulled over, rotations of sentries individually waking successors studied, all possible movements allowed for, scrupulously the plan finalised; equipment purloined and hidden.

For freedom and speed we would be scantily clad. Denim trousers, cardigan, balaclava, gloves. No footwear: but a couple of pairs of socks. That way there would be no tell-tale boot-prints!

Quite definitely we two alone knew the how and when!

To a background of snoring, with a silent handshake, we slipped out.

Luckily, not only was it dark, it was wet and windy. The wind was like music. The rain perhaps deter any perambulation of an Orderly Officer! Just everything went perfectly! Within minutes not one, but two hand-grabbed buckets of coal hidden away in the hut. Gear likewise. Nobody had been seen; nobody, we felt sure, had spotted us and no sleeping colleagues had been disturbed!

Wet clothes discarded, came the safety of beds. Despite the cold what a beautiful sleep it was too, having remained awake until time for the sortie!

Reveille! Smiles all round at the uncovering of the first bucket. Two, whoops of astonishment! Imagine! That evening, with ceremonial lighting, the hut would be thawed out! Something to really cheer the day ahead. Congratulations continued during icy ablutions and the mad scramble for First Parade! But jubilations must be contained!

The Colonel was accompanied by his most senior Training Officer, a Capt. Richards of the Gloucesters – those with the front and back badges. Front inspection completed, the two moved behind. Going through some pretence of kit adjustment, astonishingly, came a whisper from the Captain!

'A good soldier must take calculated risks'!

Oh no! How could he possibly know anything? Parade over, bewilderingly, extraordinarily, the other half of the night's escapade had received exactly the same whisper! How could our secret possibly have leaked? Particularly to the Officers Mess. And so swiftly? Fellow hutmates were just as baffled. Not a clue!

It was, and remained, a complete mystery.

That is until many months later, in an old Depot News Sheet somebody stumbled on the name of an officer who had served at the Camp a couple of years earlier – the name identical with that of one of our Hut 21 so-called 'Sapper' mates. One and the same bloke of course! A plant! Imposter! With hindsight we recalled how he had been the first to 'qualify', ostensibly, for WOSB and away! The ideal fifth-columnist! Pure, simple, dastardly deception!

As for the irony, my whole life had been spent in the Coal Trade! Must have handled hundreds of ships, thousands of wagons! Just before joining up had arranged whole trainloads for Aldershot – almost certainly including the protected coal in that Compound too!

Monkey Climb

Anyone who frequented the large NAAFI at Longmoor might have noticed, in the woods nearby, a clearing where trees were interspersed with a liberal sprinkling of telegraph poles, some with platforms atop poking still further skywards. The trees, the poles, all interconnected with ropes.

Here was the Monkey Climb! An obstacle course devised with all the ingenuity and inventiveness of Royal Engineers. Single, double and triple ropes cunningly set up, so that once having commenced there was no possible way back.

Built for Commando training, selectees from many Regiments and Corps now converged in to pit and prove themselves against this monster.

The starting point, thirty feet up, could only be reached by swarming a dangling rope. Simple for an unencumbered Tarzan. Easy, in vest and shorts, for the reasonably athletic. Clad in light battle order – pack, helmet, rifle – it was an awesome challenge! Climbing the rope to the start might be as far as some ventured before shinning down to terra-firma, to await another day.

Ropes trailed at grotesque angles. On single leads the fundamental was always to keep the feet wrapped firmly around. Hanging below, hand over hand edging headfirst, agility and strength of arms did the rest! Other ropes, one below the other were negotiated with arms and legs extended, body forming an X. Three ropes shaped to a V made the usual walking bridges.

The smaller and nimbler became the more successful 'monkeys', mastering the art of swaying so that the rifle did not impede.

Perched up there at great height figures on the ground appeared miniscule. An exercise wholly unsuited for anyone prone to dizziness.

'Vertigoes' definitely did not volunteer – which was an essential.

It was a Friday.

Emerging from the NAAFI, hearing voices above, we had interestedly wandered along as spectators. An ominous look about the sky, already a mizzle in the air, we wouldn't be long.

The highlight of the previous day had been a twelve miles in two hours forced run and march in full battle order across country: through hedges, over walls, fording rivers. Barracks in sight, forming up for the quick march to the Parade Ground.

'Come on now! Shoulders back! Heads high! March as if you're on a Royal Parade!'

Trouble was though, I'd been obliged to part with cherished old Home Guard boots. Breaking in the new ones had left heels bare of flesh, ugly and bleeding. Self applied makeshift bandages needed renewing.

Just a few minutes watching the antics on the Monkey Climb and I'd see to those heels: then precious desperately needed relief, flat on the back!

The mizzle became a drizzle. Heavy black clouds warned of a storm. About to seek shelter, the heavens opened, which was precisely the time I was spotted by Big Jock the Scots Guards P.T. Sergeant. A footballer of repute, he skippered the Depot XI.

'Hi there Jar! Do me a favour! Guested for Southampton yesterday. Sprained me ankle. Couple o' volunteers here. Take 'em over?'

Not enthusiastically, quite unthinkingly, I did the sporting thing, (if only perhaps to protect my place in his soccer team!).

Taking off, the second staging post was reached without difficulty. Urging advice and encouragement, we would next traverse a drooping single rope, the longest span of the lot. The claps of thunder must on no account disturb concentration! Then came the daddy of all storms! The wind whipped up to gale force. In almost darkness, the rain hammered down in torrents.

Those heels were aching! Stripped of the bandages what would they look like? Blast those new boots!

The split second's mental aberration was enough! Hell! My feet! They were not around the rope! Hanging by the hands, this was impossible! No chance of getting back with the rope near vertical! Came the awful realisation that were it physically possible to edge along, the other end would be near vertical too! Hands burning, arms excruciatingly tearing at the sockets, whole body quivering, there was no alternative.

'I'm coming down!'

'No! For Chris' sake No!' anxious voices called back.

The ground I knew to be rock hard with roots of felled trees. The load must be lightened. Hanging by one hand whilst shaking the rifle clear, a quick flick to remove helmet only succeeded in pushing it backwards, rim digging deep into the base of the neck.

I hit the ground. Felt nothing and wondered why. Few people were around; most had scampered for shelter. Voices however, despite the thunder, were quite clear.

'Is he dead? Listen to his heart!'

Clamouringly, others were shouting differently.

'No! No! Don't touch him!'

Dead? Me? I remember thinking. Far from it! In a tick I'll jump laughingly to my feet and ask what all the fuss was about. 'Now!' No reaction! Funny! My brain was clear. Felt no pain.

The shouting went on. 'Phone Officers Mess', 'Get the MO' and 'Telephone the Guard Room'. I'd give it another go, show 'em I was OK; had a miracle landing, couldn't feel a thing!

I must then have passed out.

Waking, reading the question in my eyes, doctors and nurses told me. 'Cambridge Military Hospital, Aldershot. But remain quite still!'

Still? What for? Surely I can move? Trying, there was no response! Apparently the comas lasted days. On each awakening, the same effort, and the same prayer. 'Not me God! Not paralysed! Please!'

First recognition was the peering face of a pal with whom many of the little triumphs and disasters of a ranker's life had been shared. Annoyingly, he was whispering, almost reverently!

'Congratulations! Depot Orders this morning. You've been promoted! Acting Unpaid Local Lance Corporal!' I got the message but don't know that he knew. Hell, why was he so untypically gentle?

Again waking, it was in a corridor immediately adjacent to the Operating Theatre; in isolation.

Life would never be the same.

Weeks later, guinea-pig to the new-fangled Army-boots-from-the-start technique, supported by pretty nurses, the first faltering steps. Could I, would I, ever be able to walk again? The long haul back had begun! Medical discharge from the Services? No, I'd stay on and sweat it out! That Commission seemed now altogether impossible.

Another hut-mate brought the news. War Office had ordered immediate destruction of the Obstacle Course. Unknown to us it had claimed too many casualties.

Well I could perhaps feel I'd done somebody a favour! And in token evidence one morale boosting solitary stripe lay where it had been left, on the bedside locker!

Mole Tunnels

Large scale hazards had been constructed, originally for Commando training. Of extreme difficulty, for volunteers only.

The Second Front had yet to come.

Those applying for Movements PO Course, a Pre-Pre-OCTU programme, were well aware completion of these obstacle pieces provided a rough and ready means of limiting the numbers selected.

All at the Battalion were on Infantry training and Classroom work, running in parallel.

Indoor study was learning something about logistics. Papers included a mass of code letters and numbers, combinations of which were learned by rote, in off-duty hours endlessly chanted together and identified. Everything had to be memorised. This in preparation for the invasion of the Continent, wherever it might be.

Many were to put such knowledge to the test on D-Day. At Arromanches and the Normandy landings, recognising Units, armaments, stores, directing these to points on the beaches, under fire.

For me, a guardian angel determined otherwise! (Remember the film 'The Longest Day'? Kenneth More played the part of Beach Landing Master, first on the beaches, contriving order out of chaos. Worth mentioning, one feels, as the general impression of Movement Control is of RTO's at Railway Stations and STO's at Seaports, seemingly on a cushy number, issuing cover chits for late arrival back to Unit!)

Mentally tired after hours in the classroom, regular square-bashing was irksome to say the least. For blokes on the PO Course positively devastating, filling in not only remaining hours of daylight but frequently well into dusk.

During lectures however, seated under cover, warm and dry, through windows we would watch those Longmoor Field Sappers, caped, heads bent forward into the wind and rain marching towards open heathland. These were the *real* Sappers! For them, timetables were unaffected by weather! A dirty and arduous life! Our sympathies went with them. Certainly we wouldn't swap places!

Way out across the moor these Sappers had created one masterpiece of an obstacle course. Underground! A maze of tunnels, or 'saps', covering an area maybe twice the size of a football pitch. Tunnels which just about allowed a man in battle gear to crawl. Some led to a fullstop; a blank wall of earth.

The whole formed a spider's web pattern, with junctions, discovered of course only by touch, offering a choice of two or three directions. No main tunnel, all saps identical, this maze had one entrance and one exit.

Claustrophobics voluntarily withdrew.

Even the toughest were apprehensive.

Some, ashen faced, visibly shaking, waited the word to go underground. One at a time, names taken, time noted, men dropped on all fours at intervals, all hoping to encounter the minimum of 'blanks'. Wriggling back wasn't easy - positively alarming should someone be met coming forward! How some of those giant heavily built types ever got through continues still to baffle!

The secret of completion was in trying to sense a generally forward direction and constantly reminding oneself not to panic. A shaft of daylight would be ahead . . . eventually!

What would have been given to get our hands on a copy plan of those mole-runs! Bribery or any suggestion of chicanery would have invited certain disaster!

Nobody in any way involved was allowed to leave the moor until the last man had been checked out. Missing a meal of no consequence! Overdue troglodytes frequently put the Rescue Squad into action.

The most scrupulous planning and supervision, the strictest safety measures, should have made it quite impossible, but happen it did! Back at Camp and purely by chance, somebody 'missing'. Rumour got round he'd been a volunteer for the Mole Tunnels.

Staff alerted, there followed one almighty frantic scramble back over the moor to that subterranean nightmare!

He'd passed out. In a blank tunnel.

Pulling and pushing, they unearthed him.

Poor chap! He didn't see daylight again.

Well, after all, five per cent casualties were permitted by the War Office.

A.B.C.A.

Occasionally Depot Daily Orders would include such an item as '19.00 hrs: ABCA Session – Main Dining Hall'.

Not compulsory, with the exception of those on duty, the RSM expected the whole Battalion to attend. Tactically it was wise to do so.

A monthly bulletin produced by the Education Corps, written by the best available journalists under War Office direction, contained articles attempting to inform, on a global basis, the whole War effort. These guidelines, hopefully, included the right amount of propaganda to stimulate morale!

Copies were limited.

Unattractive, the bulletins were intended to be studied and assimilated by whomsoever delegated to lead the sessions; the idea being to interest, inform, and encourage general discussion.

When a man doesn't know what's going on in his own home town or village he's not much concerned with problems and difficulties much more distant!

Pressure to attend ABCA's was resented by the vast majority. An imposition!

ABCA – Army Bureau of Current Affairs – had not been introduced until the War had been going some time. Many old soldiers hadn't even heard of it as some Units completely ignored its existence.

Course colleagues who used the Education Hut with its quiet atmosphere as a place for relaxation, study, and a market place for picking up Camp news, could not avoid becoming aware of ABCA issues. Small groups were positively encouraged to mull over the military, political and moral issues within its pages.

Debate was inevitable. Articulation, so essential in communication, blossomed with obligatory five-minute 'lectures', each man spontaneously discoursing on a subject, sometimes outrageously risqué, thought up on the spur of the moment. Some very off-beat morsels popped up! It was a tongue-loosening practice invaluable to the more taciturn and mono-syllabic amongst us!

Bob didn't need such exercise!

Bob was a natural, volubly over-spilling discussion and argument until well after Lights-Out, only finally to be silenced by a chorus of choice expletives from comrades screamingly anxious for precious sleep.

Bob had been a junior Trade Union official. A chip off the old block, inspired by his father's rhetoric outside the gates of The Royal Dock-yards on London River – in days long before any Dockers Charter.

Bob was good company, his quick witted Cockney humour appreciated all round. Passionate, strongly opinionated, he despised privilege, abhorred wealth. On every occasion possible would remind his listeners of a book on Economics, the first three words of which were 'Labour is wealth'. We wouldn't disagree, but he would like to claim he alone understood and spoke for the ordinary bloke. Paradoxically, ordinary blokes had been selected, he amongst them, for training as officers! Clearly, a dilemma! For dockers versus management and the Port of London Authority, substitute Privates versus Officers and the War Office!

Bob's enthusiasm for Trade Unionism up till now had remained unaffected by the constrictions of military life. He carried his gospel with him.

When the officer usually assigned to take ABCA went on leave he had already discovered that Bob would make a willing deputy.

Bob relished having such an audience. To the neo-Marxist rabble-rousing of which he was capable, the Camp's massive khaki crowd was gleefully responsive.

The officer concerned, a glutton for slipping off on regular 48-hour passes thereafter found no difficulty whatever in appointing an ABCA stand-in.

The danger was patently obvious!

Bob was a pal. Pals can be cruelly blunt!

Bob was alerted to the fact his very presence on the Course was in jeopardy. Also that the democratic process (a phrase he was particularly fond of using) demanded his dogma be challenged.

General concensus of opinion prevailed. When the next ABCA session came round, wisely, Bob was side-lined, which proved an eventual blessing for him. Extremists would not be welcomed into the Officers Mess. Great efforts were made to keep ABCA equally lively. We did Bob a favour, though it was almost too late!

Denied his platform Bob's confidential ratings must have increased considerably, though as things turned out he was relegated to the next incoming Course, so it was understood, 'for further assessment'.

Poor old Bob! Separated from we his mates of Hut 21 he did see the light, came to terms with military conformity, and went on to a Royal Engineers commission.

But when the 1945 'khaki' vote put the Socialists firmly into power, Bob swept into Parliament with a thumping majority as member for his beloved Bermondsey! He very nearly lost a War-time commission but all along knew where his future lay!

For the Army, ABCA sessions may or may not have been a good thing. For Bob they provided a stamping ground; a platform for proving his talent, a talent which ultimately took him to Cabinet office.

• • •

Forty-five years on, isn't it strange how so very few comrades of those days have either been seen or heard of, unless, like Bob, shot to prominence? (County Regiments of the line, such as our local Suffolks and Norfolks excepted, where, having returned to their roots, men still bump into each other).

For many years his Party's Chief Whip, Bob mellowed. Most surprisingly, Bermondsey dropped him in favour of a young, extreme Left, avowed Militant. Was his name Tatchell? I'm not sure. What I am sure of is that at the same age Bob would have gobbled him up for breakfast!

And a little confession. Having originated that resistance to ABCA monopoly, things haven't changed much. Uncommitted and independent, political goals not for me . . . an unpaid Parish Pump seat suits fine. And there's a goodly number of ordinary Ex-Service people in the Local Council Chamber. Much more fun than Westminster, and just as rewarding, Bob!

Now in the Upper Chamber, Bob is 'My Lord'.

The ghosts of Hut 21 will echo that!

Wrotham

'Come home Dad seriously ill Marjorie'. The telegram received by Camp Signals had been steered to the Sherwood Foresters, and very belatedly passed by a disbelieving HQ office Sergeant to an even more sceptical Sergeant-Major, who dismissively tossed it to me.

'In the Army, boy, you ain't got no farvver, you ain't got no muvver, and you ain't got no bruvvers and sisters neiver!!' he declared.

The first week had been spent with the 8th Battalion of the Sherwoods and the next four on gruelling infantry training with the Leicesters. We had now shuttlecocked back to the Sherwoods.

This was Pre-OCTU, Wrotham, in Kent.

Punishment Centre? It was a veritable Alcatraz for rankers having the big-headed temerity to seek a commission!

Always an awkward day, of all days it had to be a Saturday!

And Wrotham was in that very sensitive area where security had limited travel to a radius of five miles. The telegram was from Manchester! Prospects of compassionate leave, zero!

However, hours later, having desperately lobbied, and almost convinced, all up to the rank of Colonel that Marjorie really was my kid sister, really did live in Manchester, that quite definitely it was not a bogus wire from either a mistress or a crony, the strict travel limitation was reluctantly relaxed! Assured a place on the same Course would not be jeopardised, a seven-days Pass was in my hands.

Not unusually, I was stony broke. Not a penny! Sapper's pay made sure of that! Came the almighty performance of raising a £3 advance in pay, alarmingly delaying departure.

However, eventually, I was hareing along to the 'Vigo' Pub busstop: on the way to London and the North.

The Euston train, with its weekend travellers, was overcrowded; jammed with Service people standing, squatting, lying down, amongst a welter of kit and weaponry. I joined them, forcing space on the corridor floor.

My father had survived two heart attacks. Could not speak. Fixing me with glazed eyes I knew he had noted the khaki: wished enlightenment on the strips of white ribbon on the shoulder straps. For hours holding his gnarled cold hands I did the only thing one could. Overtired and physically shattered for months, after a couple of days and nights' constant vigil there was little resistance to Matron's persuasion. I was lying down in a small room at the end of the Ward. Something instinctive got me to my feet. Fighting against sleep was not unfamiliar. I knew I had to go back.

Half-a-dozen doctors and nurses were crowded around. My Dad was attempting to raise himself: being forcibly restrained.

The jabs finished him off.

I had been constantly trained to kill. One long Course actually called The Spirit of the Bayonet.

Here, before my eyes, was a killing, albeit in mercy! My own father! Medical staff scattered in confusion as I reached him.

Funeral over, it was back to Wrotham.

Back to the killing business!!

The long unfortunate absence made it imperative for extra physical effort to catch up. I dare not break down! Having refused Medical Discharge out of the Service, talked and walked myself out of hospitals, somehow I just had to keep going for that commission.

Many considerate employers and certainly all Local Authorities continued to pay salaries to men in the ranks, who thereby were quite content to stay there although many would have made damn good officers. To them Army pay merely beer money.

'Anyone joining up'll get no bloody help from this firm!' had threatened my own blunt Managing Director.

How can one describe a Pre-OCTU?

No esprit-de-corps. No regimental pride. No feeling of 'belonging'. No teamwork. Little or no camaraderie. How could there be? It was all a case of every man for himself, devil take the hindmost.

Its aim was the physical, mental, and psychological destruction of the individual. The rooting out of 'unsuitable material' and no consideration allowed to interfere. Sadistically broadcast, the intent was repeatedly, unashamedly, clear! To provoke, to invoke, the dreaded pronouncement: 'RTU' – Returned to Unit.

Somehow, I wasn't . . . and OCTU, a possibility!

• • •

Some twenty years after the War had finished I nudged the car towards and around Wrotham Hill, stopping here and there to explore.

Nature had long since taken over!

Maybe memory had let me down?

Perhaps I hadn't penetrated the wild growth sufficiently?

No sign existed of the Camp which so very dramatically determined the future lives of those who had been there! Not even a single concrete slab which might once have taken a nissen hut! Nothing!

In the densely wooded area the air was still, and, eerily, no birdsong.

Perhaps that camp of a thousand terrors really had been just a bad dream?

But the 'Vigo' Pub still stood there. You who frequented it might subconsciously have directed your feet towards the site of the Pre-OCTU which so many shudder to recall yet cannot forget. For me, visiting the Vigo's bar was out of the question. A cup of tea at the NAAFI something of a luxury, although this easily dismissed from mind when exercising atop the escarpment and the order for ten minutes' break called. One remembered the sheer folly in attempting to career downhill and clamber back in time. The very fittest were frequently unsuccessful – beaten by the length of the NAAFI queue!

Yes, Wrotham was pure purgatory. Why had I returned? Some Freudian, inexplicable urge?

Dry and crackling bracken underfoot alone disturbed the uncanny silence. But of course this *was* strange! That sojourn of the past had been in winter, and the abiding memory of mud! Mud, MUD everywhere! Mud which stuck! Mud which stank!

Clearly, the first day of reporting here came flooding back. Men assigned to 'our' hut wearing flashes of an extraordinary diversity of Regiment and Corps! Veterans of Dunkirk: battle-decorated Desert Rats of the Eighth Army: seasoned regulars from crack outfits. Every conceivable rank, though about to be stripped. Incongruously, a Welsh Guards R.S.M.!

And the resolution, vividly recalled, never to be dazzled, never to be left behind, by this intimidating galaxy of talent!

'Our' hut was one of three or four on the lower perimeter, surrounded by a sea of mud which inevitably invaded. A narrow rough brick track had at one time led to this enclave but long since submerged.

The nissen's front door also served as exit. The back door had a special purpose! Facing this, before parading, men jockeyed for position, edging forward in pairs, until, shoulder to shoulder, came the performance of urinating out! That rear ground nobody trod, ever!

Clean boots basic and paramount, in these diabolic conditions a special technique evolved. Laces tied together, boots were slung about the neck and anchored to some part of the equipment: gaiters stuffed into pockets: trouser bottoms, creases neatly folded over, tucked into socks.

Habitually so, with deliberate steps to avoid catastrophe, one squelched through mud until reaching upper concrete paths of the

Camp. Short lengths of stick scraped off the larger lumps before feet, mud an' all, went into those precious clean boots, sticks replaced conveniently into the ground. We were ready then for the 'bull' of the sacred Parade Ground! There was no possible alternative.

But surely, I mused, there should be more important things to remember about the place than such uncou' squalor?

No-ones fate became known until all the miserable weeks ended. The failure rate remained a mystery. 'Insufficient RE officer casualties' – so they blandly said at the time – 'choose for your future from Pay, Pioneer, Service, or Signals Corps'. Sappers and Pioneers such close brothers-in-arms for me the choice easy, determining as it did the next challenge, the next destination, OCTU.

Now, all these years later, very occasionally one meets up with an ex-Serviceman who, with a choke in the voice might say 'What? Wrotham Pre-OCTU! You? YOU were actually at WROTHAM?!!'

Crude and obscene. Yes, that was Pre-OCTU, though on first arrival our lot should really have guessed what to expect when a Drill Sergeant's greeting clearly spelled out the unimportance of Cadets. Never, ever, to be forgotten!

'You'se blankety so-called blankety gentlemen – you'se blankety well nithin' but blankety sh--!'

Snowdonia

A baptism.
Simulation of the real thing.

Fear? Apprehension? Not really!

All the tiresome hours spent on Rifle Ranges, with stints in the butts, had been by the book, ultra-safety in mind and under strict supervision.

This next seven days promised to be scarey, including exposure to the withering 'live' fire of rifles, machine guns, mortars and whatever else could be unleashed. All Hell, so it was said, would be thrown at us!

The numbering, dressing, quick marching, slow marching, eyes front, thumbs down seam of trousers, slope arms, present arms, move to the right in threes, about turns and 'shuns of everlasting square bashing had achieved its purpose.

Now, the cream of Drill Sergeants were oozing justifiable pride and satisfaction in having cajoled, bullied and honed their charges to near perfection! Files of men, robots, moved as one, unthinkingly, unswervingly.

Individualism long since surrendered, bodies, physically and mentally tired, were but as lumps of clay in the hands of a potter – stretched, pummelled, thoroughly beaten! The clay had been moulded, ready for the kiln. After firing, some pieces would not emerge whole and be scrapped.

'Live?' So what? It was but an extension of the many dummy runs, and if a stray one happened to be picked up, well, it could mean a long, long blissful rest, somewhere!

The real anxiety, the real fear, was 'RTU'.

Nobody could be free of that!

An abrupt end to months of agonising toil! The ignominy of failure!

Niggling and uppermost in all minds, this held far more terror than any inaccurate fire could bring!

As threatened, the week brought all the expected, and the unexpected, scheduled and unscheduled. Under such simulated activity the only distinction could be extinction!

Friday brought the grand climax.

All the grind, all the techniques of simulated experience concentrated in a massive full-scale exercise with leadership, planning, decision-making in the hands of Cadets, chosen at random.

Mission outlined, advance troops, 'O' group, rifle and machine gun cover parties, mortar teams had been briefed, re-briefed, ready to go.

Foolishly, a Military Training Officer had been given the tip-off some General would be observing.

'Shouldn't tell you this' he confided 'but the actual target will be that cleft, eleven o'clock, across the valley there, to the right of those isolated trees. Now put on a dam' good show!'

Permanent staff, already in position, primed the props. The thunder of detonated mines, mortar fire, rattle of machine guns, release of smoke canisters, brilliance of tracer bullets, and the exploding of many spectacular earpiercing fireworks, set the stage.

Watches, supply issue, synchronised, at scheduled 'let battle commence' zero hour, the cast moved off to play out appointed roles.

Swelteringly, in high summer's sunshine, heavily laden in full battle-order, men were crawling along hugging the ground, breaking and making sudden dashes to the next cover. Sweat and smoke! Irritated eyes! Parched throats!

Our cover party had set out on a circuitous detour. To remain unseen, seemingly for an eternity, scrambling through and over obstacles which, in any hostile country, geographically could not be possible!

Organisers, secreted in hide-outs en route, joyfully added to the cacophony by hurtling more and more crackerjacks and incendiaries into our midst.

Sweating, clothes stuck to the body. Heads throbbing, helmets forbidden to be removed, even momentarily. Flat on bellies, at last reaching the highest ground, we had been following a sheeptrack and occasional rough scrub.

The whole of the valley now in view, bringing up the rear, and last to drop into position, I was at the end of the line. Placing rifle in readiness for firing from the left shoulder (which wasn't in the script!) quite by chance I glanced to the rear. What a surprise!

Looking me straight in the face was General Dyer!

He placed a finger to pursed lips. Two others were with him.

Crawling from the very scrub we had just used as cover!

If this was a play, then came the denouement!

Accent recognisable, it was the voice of 'Tissle' – he came from Oswaldtwistle.

'No it isn't' he was loudly protesting 'HE said it was near those other isolated trees, further over!'

Signal not given, a gaffe of monumental proportions! Agreements and disagreements along the line echoed to and fro.

The General, who must have been inwardly exploding, lay doggo!

Battle noises grew to a tremendous roar.

Textbook methods of attack unfolded.

Our cover party merrily blazed away.

Inevitably, 'the enemy' was eliminated!

Though fully and excellently camouflaged, normal descent was not for us. The Cadet-cum-temporary Platoon Commander played it safe. 'The rules' demanded cover and more cover, crawling and still more crawling, retracing the way up! Heat overpowering, energy draining away, this was something most would never again have to endure! In the real thing we reckoned we'd have stayed put and had a smoke before chancing it directly downhill, on foot!

In a state of collapse we flopped down at the reporting point to await all on the stunt and the prescribed check on returnees.

I kept my mouth shut!

The MTO's zeal had backfired, horribly!

The General was livid!

Very, very briefly, he condemned the whole 'battle' as a bloody cheat, crucified everybody concerned and stormed off!

We gathered a few heads rolled.

'Tissle' disappeared - R.T.U.'d for one!

Precisely as anticipated, casualties were not inflicted by '*live*' ammo!

Lobby Lud

In far off pre-War days seaside holidaymakers were invited to advance flourishing a newspaper to declare 'You are Lobby Lud! I claim the News Chronicle five pound prize!'

Or was it ten pounds?

At Battle School, it was Lobby, though himself injured, who helped drag me bodily across the slopes of Snowdon to the Halfway Hotel.

Officially 'walking wounded', he and I had been left behind to guard the bivvy camp when all in the contingent had been called out on a night exercise.

The rain started. Should we grab capes or leave them protecting our foxholes? An electric storm, with torrential rain soaking us to the skin resolved the question immediately. The capes stayed put.

On the qui vive, sentry duty dare not be shirked. Spies, vicious spies, in the shape of Training Officers and their cohorts might launch an 'attack' and wreak havoc. It was vital to look out for 'enemy patrols'!

Luckily for me, good Fleet Street man as he was, Lobby proved marvellous company. Extremely articulate, he talked me through pain barriers and the night, determined to keep me awake.

Throughout the dark hours it bucketted down. At dawn, comrades returned, and what a farce, actually attempting to march! Slithering and stumbling, curses rang out as rifles went keeling into the mud. We were to learn their night had been spent on a flat-on-the-belly mine-pricking, mine-detection, stunt!

What a relief to see that bedraggled column staggering back! Thank God, camp guard duty was over!

Unable to remain awake I made for my fox-hole. It was three-quarters full of water. Blissfully I dropped into it, oblivious to all.

Within minutes however, and most unusually, the whole camp had been condemned. Sited on a slope, every foxhole waterlogged!

Roused and hauled out of the ground by Lobby, together we followed the crowd, maybe a couple of miles, to a farm. On the upper floor of an out-building, a miracle, bales of straw! Little room to stretch out fully, but heaven!

Glorious luxury however promptly disturbed!

Another awakening. More commotion!

'Those not in possession of all kit, go and collect!'

In complete stupor, along with the many others who had left those useless capes behind, it was another hour's stumbling through the dark and merciless rain before the last to return, the lame Charlies, were picking their way over prostrate bodies in an attempt to find somewhere to kip. Hitting the hay, in a squatting position, as if poleaxed, sleep came solidly. Though a few hours to Reveille it seemed immediate to me. Not so for others. There had been pandemonium! Hordes of rats scampering around in protest at the intrusion!

He who selected the bivvy site paid the penalty. The cruelty of 'RTU' remained effective though but only hours to go. On this occasion there was little sympathy!

Talk of hospital arrangements for casualties brought a frightening chill. Persuasive advice met with positive and determined resistance. The handicapped Lobby held on with me. Certainly we would not go voluntarily. Fortunately we made it to the end.

And what a week that turned out to be!

Constantly on the move. Ever open to the elements. Crawling along watercourses. Long, long days toiling in temperatures approaching the eighties. Clambering up scree, cross rifle fire at heels to ensure speed. The unequal struggle to keep rifle and kit clean. Over shockingly precarious rope bridges. Not one night's full sleep. Wilful non-arrival of promised hot char during night exercises. Sans all hygiene facilities. Regular unexpected 'live' bombardments overhead. Direct up-and-over mountain forays. Always in battle kit. Always taking a turn at carrying a machine gun or ammo box. Always short of food. Perpetually exhausted!

When the real thing came, if it did, at least we knew what to expect! All so painfully endured, but, we reasoned together, surely in these enlightened times Generals would handle men better than this on the battlefield? Were we really to expect another Somme? Or another Passchendale? When men overstretched, overtired, overhungry, completely unready for fighting, had become such easy cannon fodder?

'Going over the top?' Be-ribboned Infantry colleagues included, it was unanimously agreed those who had prepared this 'live' School already *had*!

Bodies had been pushed in fury of mind over matter with sheer, almost inhuman, effort and determination. Voices around had urged the stumbling on. Younger, fitter, men in the true spirit of comradeship had shoved and propelled the middle-aged who clearly should never, ever, have been subjected to such profane extremes of endurance. And the whole saga nothing but pretence!

The real battle was very private, very individual!

'The difficult we do immediately, the impossible takes just a bit longer!' no more a mere catchphrase but the self evident truth! Though at times we would willingly, quite happily, have died, we could and would take whatever came our way!

This Live Battle School daily parody of bayonets fixed, careering uphill and downhill screaming obscenities was nearing merciful release. The last day's final assault would allegedly drive 'the enemy' to the beaches, trapped! Up in the heights, at some wonderful vantage point, we were looking down at a glorious panoramic coastline. Ahead was Penmaenmawr! The beach-huts there had been the base from which this frenetic week had started, and would finish. Like a vast mirror, the sea reflected high summer's brilliant sunshine; white foam spread itself along the glistening firm shore.

Grown men, experienced men, wept tears of joy! Couldn't wait. Down there, thank God, the end loomed. To take and surround the beach it was to be a massed non-stop advance. Within minutes, all over!

We charged downhill.

Exhilaratingly, without premeditation, textbook methods were disregarded. On, on, the charge continued; dumping helmets, packs, rifles in the beach-huts, on, on, across the firm sand and into the cooling briny, fully clad!

What indescribable ecstacy! What joy! Tension over, men plunged and plunged again. Whoops of laughter! Coming up in a mass of bodies, rubbing tired eyes clear, it was to become face to face with Lobby Lud.

'To Hell with all your fivers!' I laughed.

'Amen to that!' echoed a beaming, splashing, Lobby.

Pain cannot be aggregated. All there is in the whole world can only be concentrated in one body. Only endured with real friendship. And a helping hand.

Lobby Lud had given me that. I offered mine, and we shook.

Wherever you are Lobby, Thanks!

Thanks a lot, mate!

D-Day and Mushrooms

'There is a destiny which shapes our ends'. How true!

It was an accepted certainty that when the time came yours truly would be amongst the first on the beaches.

Vast amounts of bewilderingly complex detail, combinations of numbers and code letters, had been laboriously memorised – defying all use of helpful mnemonics devised in other aspects of training. The whole sphere of logistics reflected in these codes, a brainstore totally useless if not deployed at the outset of the Second Front . . . the invasion of the Continent.

There were no doubts. Draftees drawn from all parts of the Army, and the Canadian Army, were aware, as the guessing time drew near, we, the current strength of Checkers within Movement Control, with the key information freshly in mind, would take precedence over those who had earlier gone through the same Course. 'Our lot' would be the very core of Movements – thrown in at the beginning!

This however was to reckon without fate and normal unpredictability of Service life!

The joining of a special Course, hospitalisation, deferment of Boards, eventual WOSB (three intensive physical days adding to Sick Parade attendance) all contributed to threaten the absolute certainty of D-Day involvement. Even so, as the weeks and months slipped by, possibility remained. A few days of OCTU to go and D-Day still unknown.

It was a bright, clear morning. Suddenly a deep increasingly deafening roar in the blue skies above presaged the day. This was it! Thousands of planes as far as the eye could see, steadily heading south. Elsewhere it would be the same. Vast, purposeful, armadas in formation, destined to rendezvous with timely precision over the Channel!

The roar went on . . . and on! Right now my Movements buddies, close pals, would be going over – probably already there! May good luck be with them!

Familiar faces flashed through the mind. Invasion vows made to each other: promises, my own personal promises, now beyond fulfilment! Here was I, quite alone, with time to think, safe in Lincolnshire engaged on a routine 'Handing over/Taking over' admin exercise! With a shrug, the inconsequential findings were scribbled down. 'Toilet Block: W.C. No.4 – Chain missing. Door damaged'.

Well, there it was! What a load of rubbish!

How utterly ridiculous!

Men, my friends, were dying!

Symbolically, don't ask me why, I stood on the WC pedestal and flushed the chainless cistern, unformed prayers my only contribution. Why had the fates spared me from certain mayhem?

Commissioned, it was to arrive in a Kent village.

Infantry had moved off to board landing craft.

Everything not required for battle had been left behind. Tentage, kitchens, ammunition, equipment, clothing, tarpaulins, food supplies and stores of every description. Briefing had been to dismantle and collect the lot.

References transposed to map, the amazing number, the concentration, of those camps was mind boggling!

A huge number of men assembled, Sergeants were seeking instructions from two very raw, newly-made-up, one pippers. Vast nominal roll split down the middle, two massive working parties were agreed.

Programme devised, a fleet of RASC-driven lorries lined up to carry Pioneers all over Kent.

At sites visited, flagpoles stood bare alongside notice boards which but hours before had carried famous flashes. Beyond rustic entrance gates in perfect working order, stood a plethora of sectional buildings – living huts, ablution blocks, latrines; tall water towers, and most other impedimenta of camp life. Silent and abandoned. No indication of the bustling previous occupation. Any interested foreign agent would have been totally disappointed!

Reaching each camp, men were dropped.

Map references led into extensive country estates: vast acres of beauty where for centuries privacy had been jealously protected; historic tranquility momentarily disturbed!

The tremendous number of privately owned estates was astonishing. Acres and acres of unseen Kent! Very much England's *unknown* green and pleasant land.

Now in Normandy, infantrymen from cities and towns of the industrial North and the Midlands must have marvelled at this glorious rolling countryside, this Eden, wholly unaware men of Kent and Kentishmen themselves had seen nothing of it!

With the scheduled clearances, and when restored to former normality, wealthy landowners would be paid generous compensation. With the average ranker's financial difficulties and traumas in mind this was disturbing. Supremely ignorant of such things, one felt sure the landed privileged could not possibly comprehend the paradox!

A routine developed.

Accumulated stores were soon being ferried to distant Ordnance Depots. Sergeants, bless 'em all, had everything under control. Shortly, it would never be suspected these secret places had harboured a vast invasion force.

Subject to the day's demands, for me, at each morning's mass departure, it was a case of climbing at random on any vehicle; from some remote hive of activity diverting the first loaded lorry on to another camp; and so continue on wide ranging tours.

On the second morning, a whispered invitation from one Sergeant to first accompany the working party for 'his' estate, was intriguing. 'We'll look after you!' he promised '. . . and well!'

Arriving, figures promptly fanned out over grassland and hillocks, disappearing into the distance. Clearly, there was method about this!

Before long, smoke from a wood fire drifted amiably on the fresh morning air, delighting the nostrils. Came a wave from the Sergeant, and I joined him. By that fire.

In heavy large frying pans sizzled the largest, scrumptuous, mushrooms imaginable, and more than enough for everybody!

The whole contingent gathered round. What a luscious feast! Swilled down by the sweetest hot char!

The brilliant sunshine, the delightful pastoral setting, the scented wood fire, the laughter, what glorious precious moments these were! Above the happy banter larks were in full song! Very near perfection! A time to savour, and remember!

What a contrast with events across the Channel!

Of all the Movement Control Sappers I knew who went over on D-Day, since then I have met but one. He talked only of the good times: kept mum about the bad!

These days when I go down to Legion meetings of a Friday night, men now getting old reminisce about Arromanches, Mulberry and first Normandy landings. Respectfully, I listen.

Amongst these warriors, when occasionally pressed to reveal personal involvement, I do know the acute of hearing have puzzlingly put a strangely mumbled response down to the beginnings of senile dementia!

'Er . . . Number Four Lavatory chain . . . and, O Yes . . . Mushrooms!'

Grenades with Mustard

Under the Emperor Claudius, Roman Legions had a settlement at Richborough.

In their footsteps now stood a purpose-built Royal Marines Training Establishment, and, opposite this, the rotting remains of a hutted First World War Camp into which Pioneer Units had been dumped to await shipment across the Channel. Archaeologists had it on record those Romans enjoyed infinitely more comfortable quarters!

The old historic harbour, with its long neglected mudflats had also been pressed into service. So called secret constructional work noisily proceeding. Strange steel tanks floated alongside the rickety staithes: these commonly to become known as LCT's and LCP's (Landing Craft Tanks and Landing Craft Personnel).

For a period wholly unknown, off-the-cuff training schedules were obliged to be thrown together to keep all troops fully occupied.

A nearby Rifle Range conveniently provided the main activity.

Within the camp itself a huge sandy hole suggested it could have been used for a specific purpose in that previous War. Here every man would, and must, be directed to throw at least one live hand grenade.

It was the idea of 'Mustard'. Training staff had accorded him the nickname. To him everything was a must. Enthusiastically slipped into the programme, quite naturally 'Mustard' was invited to get things under way.

Preliminary enquiries showed few Sergeants, drastically less Officers, had ever pulled a pin 'live' and were in no haste to do so. The mass of men, hearing what was afoot, showed similar disinclination!

Mustard could not come to terms with this.

'For Pete's sake' he would say 'What's the good of having hand grenades if people go round actually admitting they've only messed about with dummies?'

Corporals working in the ramshackle Camp HQ, privy to these things, spread the word that the extremely heavy Requisition Note put into Ordnance for live grenades had been officially queried.

From the outset it was no surprise there was a marked shortage of names for essential supervision. Undeterred, Mustard pressed on.

There was, however, no lack of working parties down at the pit to bring some reality to the constructions outlined on Mustard's rough sketchplan.

Quickly under way were the sand-bagged circular walls, the protected entrance and exit runs, and the digging of a deep rear trench for emergencies. This digging inspired considerable conjecture.

'No Man's Land' into which the grenades would be tossed was fenced off and heavily plastered with 'Keep Out' signs. Directional arrows appeared in abundance, strategically planted for the safety of the most ignorant. Over a hillock, the assembly and waiting areas clearly defined. Mustard was a stickler for detail. Nothing was left to chance. A proliferation of red flags topped out the scene.

To Mustard's frustration and contempt came the revelation that only a small percentage of all ranks had thrown even a dummy! He fumed and cursed Red Tabs responsible! To christen the Pit wished he could have the whole thumping lot shoved into his out-of-bounds circular enclosure!

'Right!' he snorted, 'No risks! The programme will be doubled! Dummy throwing first!'

Company Training Officers took the backlash. Non-stop dawn to dusk dummy sessions allocated and hastened through, Mustard growlingly in attendance urging speed and proper compilation and preservation of records. It was all a bustling business, vastly different to the familiar, more leisurely pace of the Rifle Range. All around were made to understand this was a horrible waste of time. Child's play! Mustard wanted it finished. To get on with the original idea.

That time came.

Each company was served a copy of 'Live' booking dates and times.

The tempo changed dramatically!

Allowing only one man at a time in the throwing position it became a tedious affair with inevitable long waiting periods. Hanging around with too long to think men became dangerously restless. Not just with boredom. With fright. Threatening words from Sergeants fortunately avoided near mutiny!

With each passing day the press-ganged supervisory duty roster became more and more diminished as embarkation leaves, postings away, convenient sicknesses, preferences for rifle and machine gun duties, and other vacillations, all conspired to rob Mustard of support.

Regular news of strange happenings down at the Pit did little to encourage would-be volunteers. The number of fumbled, dropped 'lives' picked up and hurled into that deep rear trench by Mustard became common knowledge.

Time and again Mustard was obliged to relieve a near-hysterical man of a metal object which somehow had become stuck to the palm of the hand!

News of the expected mass move delayed, current Richborough legions must somehow continue to be kept occupied. Totally committed and often unaccompanied, Mustard carried on, as a matter of routine regularly picking up and disposing of fumbled grenades.

Hundreds of names were still not ticked off those Nominal Rolls. Company commanders gleefully relied on slotting in large numbers of men for whole mornings, whole afternoons, sometimes whole days, into the Throwing Pit's assembly area. To fill in time they could come back next day if necessary!

Mustard was well aware of the absence of care for his own personal safety, but he would not leave any Sergeant to the follies and stupidities of terrified beginners.

The pressure was getting him down.

We gathered he'd requested all records to be scrutinized for anyone officially authorised in grenade-throwing. These ordered to join him! A 'Nil Return' confirmed to Mustard the unbelievable statistic. In that vast Camp he was the only one!

'What an Army!' he groaned, 'What a shambles!'

In arranging those bookings for the Pit Mustard did it personally. I happen to know it gave him much pleasure making those visits to all the Company offices.

He seemed to know everybody, and when a little pressure needed applying not averse to calling in on the Colonel. They seemed to get on well together.

It became clear Mustard hated routine if it could be avoided. Doing the same thing over and over again, day after day, not in his line, so he repeatedly told us. He went berserk!

'I'm bloody well sick and tired of this lot! Sod the whole blasted Pit!' he announced.

We wondered how he could possibly withdraw.

Hundreds had still not thrown a 'live'.

He'd obviously made up his mind.

But it came as a bit of a surprise to see how.

There it was on the following morning's Daily Orders.

'Drawn from all Resident Companies, Officers, Warrant Officers and Sergeants named below to parade at 08.00 hrs. and proceed to Royal Marines Depot, Deal, for the purpose of being trained and certified in the conduct of Live Hand Grenade Instruction'.

Challenged, Mustard observed he'd merely asked the Colonel to sign a request addressed to Ordnance for the Camp's Ammunition

Stores to be relieved of the remaining stock of live hand grenades as 'surplus to requirements'.

And the day after, another surprise on Daily Orders.

Mustard detailed as over-all Richborough Camp Sports & Welfare Officer!

I told you he got on well with the Colonel.

He moved in and found himself a small corner at Camp HQ.

Jokingly, we asked him what his first job would be. The answer came without hesitation.

'Must quickly scour the whole Camp. Knock together a soccer team which will slaughter those Royal Marines across the road!'

He did just that!

Mustard and his grenades!

Everybody knows many thousands never had the opportunity of firing a shot in anger. Many, many more didn't throw a hand grenade either, whether in anger or not. But that wasn't Mustard's fault.

Really, he was a man after my own heart.

Got to know him very well. Played in his soccer eleven.

If he didn't blow himself to bits before 1945 shouldn't be at all surprised to hear he went through the rest of his days saying 'I must' . . . deftly throwing a few 'lives' here and there whenever necessary!

Metaphorically speaking, of course!

Courts-Martial

The Royal Marines Barracks, Deal.

A weeks posting to this famous establishment for the express purpose of observing Courts-Martial procedures left the firm conviction that Military Law was far and away much more genuine, much more satisfactory, than Civil Law ever could be.

If a man was found guilty without any doubt he was!

One niggle however, remained.

Was the justice correctly meted out, carried through in an acceptably civilised way at those special secret places – the Detention Centres? Was the Judge Advocate General's Department alive to, and dealing with, the more than suspected level of sadism, which lingered in the mind?

In all, the Court Sitting was a three week affair.

The most common crime appeared to be the personally inflicted injury of shooting off the trigger finger, which mostly happened immediately prior to a Unit's overseas departure.

One marvelled at the armament expert's highly technical knowledge; his demonstrations and exposés of how a rifle could be fired by accident. How astonishing for we amateurs to discover that well-known standard manufacture rifles, general issue, indeed had a proclivity to go off should the butt end hit the ground or whatever, in a particular way! Man's best friend!

Everything remotely contributory was put under the microscope. All the procedures of issuing and returning ammunition to Stores minutely investigated and frequently challenged; responsibilities for 'one left up the spout' scrupulously pursued!

Certainly the Court bent over backwards in its quest to discover the flimsiest cause, anything at all, to support the inevitability of the inexplicable!

Fascinating in themselves, pleas of mitigation brought the manifold reasons why men should wish to inflict upon themselves permanent loss of a digit finger. Family problems, unfaithfulness of a wife, blitzed and broken homes, financial worries, bullying, nervous breakdowns, cowardice. The whole depressing gamut unhurriedly, studiously, described, listened to, and carefully mulled over.

Such a revelation and insight into the fallibilities of human nature!

What could not be guessed however was to later discover that the entry into one's records of those magical words 'General Courts-

Martial Course, Royal Marines, Deal' was tantamount to being a legal beagle! Regarded thereafter as having been, if not a barrister,then at least a solicitor, in civil life! Quite a handicap!

From being a normal Sports and Welfare Officer – the two duties automatically went together – the role quite unexpectedly took on new dimensions.

The first thing which dawned was that King's Regulations could be totally misconstrued, meaning different things to different people. Such a massive, complex tome could bewilder and confuse! Nobody, not even the professional clever Charlies could master that lot!! Items in isolation, like those contradictory texts from the Old Book itself, would surely perplex the most knowledgeable!

Events were to show this to be so. The most outrageous interpretations of 'KR's', expressed with profound conviction invariably 'baffled'! Yes, the proverbial Three B's did actually work!

Postings to a number of Companies might well be explained by having been thrown into this Courts-Martial business. Maybe some of us were only too well aware we were civilians in uniform. And also well aware normal commonsense approaches to given situations would not please the military purist. These postings naturally tended to expand the number of men personally known who had need to seek the ear of a Welfare Officer, and with some peculiar turn-ups.

Such as the occasion, when, having defended one miscreant, we had both been posted away. Some time later, in the Hamburg area, word came through the same man had requested my attendance as his Defending Officer . . . again. Except under very special circumstances such requests had to be honoured. His whereabouts were distant; the Court Sitting even more so; which involved hitching a round journey of some hundreds of miles. Detail of the case long since forgotten, not so the tempting, wilful, Defence interruption at a critical time, causing panic to the Prosecutor and more particularly the Chairman! The latter, always a pukka lawyer, splutteringly tutored on when Defence could and could not speak. Profuse apologies for ignorance accepted, the required damage had been done! Challenging a blatant untruth at legally the wrong time short-circuited proceedings by an hour at least, thanks, as one member of the Court was overheard to say on dispersal 'to that bloody ignorant Defence bloke'!

The rascal got a reasonable sentence, so everybody was happy!

Really though, the very first Court-Martial involvement was to prove the best remembered. Up for trial was an old sweat. A regular. Had once been in a proud well-known Regiment. The case, persistent, serious, AWOL.

Interviewing him in the glasshouse, all crime space in his AB64 had long since been taken up. Two extra sheets had been pasted in, packed tight with a variety of misdemeanours; nothing evil or violent.

Listening to his long story, quite obviously his history had worked like compound interest, attracting more and more indictments. He was past caring what happened to him. Bugger the Army!

To my surprise he had a pleasant personality. Not unintelligent, not a crook, here was a man who was his own worst enemy. What's more he knew it! The veritable likeable rogue! Who'd fought in the desert, been through the mill, had stripes. Once more in the sweet violets!

With denial of leave to visit a twice bombed-out mother he had scarpered and came perilously near being classified as a deserter.

There seemed little hope.

By his own admission he'd tried, at some time or other, the whole repertoire of cock and bull stories. The only possibility would be a plea of mitigation. He agreed. and was genuinely appreciative.

So there I was at the Hearing, drawing on years of amateur dramatics indulged in during more youthful days, pleading, trembling, choking. The emotive peroration spilled out; all of course rehearsed. Amazingly it seemed the Court was almost convinced the man had been more sinned against than sinning. Punishment was token. The man most grateful. But the Group Colonel furious when the result made known to him. He'd wanted at least two years – to be rid of him, virtually for ever!

That theatrical performance landed me another posting, and to another Group!

By one of those strange Army quirks, in the same Company, in due course came the same old soldier!

Vacancies current, and with no outstanding candidates, to test his proffered allegiance, I suggested he be entrusted with a stripe. The O.C. was stunned. No! No! The Colonel wouldn't stand for it! Well, what about hush-hush Local Acting Un-paid, experimental for a month, by which time NCO's would have sussed him out or he himself might voluntarily pack it in? Not happy, the Major agreed.

The weeks ticked by. Embarkation Leaves were in full swing, Overseas variety. Grinding training always the order of the day, relief came in organised social activity.

At a ridiculously overcrowded Sandwich hostelry a Darts match against RAF Manston was being enjoyed. Pushing through the melee to a protest of spilled pints, a man in full kit reached the ochie.

'Buy you a pint sir?' he said eagerly

'Why should you?'
'But I'm back sir!'
'So?'
'Back! Back from leave sir!'
'Enjoy yourself?'
'Yes. But first time ever sir!'
'First time what?'
'Back from leave on time! Since joined up!'
'OK. Half-pint! Have one on me later though!'
Delightedly, off he went, returning with the pint, and scrambling to produce his AB64 as evidence.
'Yes' Yes! I know! Thirteen years of AWOL!'
It was a very important occasion – an achievement, for him – and he had reason to be happy! But would it last, stripe or no stripe?
'Told you I wouldn't let you down sir!' he beamed.
It was my turn to throw for a winning double.
I missed of course!
Well, I thought, in the greater game everything's a bit of a gamble. Calculated risks had to be taken. And why not?

• • •

Many months passed.
A very junior subaltern, on BLA active service, in my hands an urgent field telegram direct from 2nd Army HQ with instructions to prepare for immediate expected landing of enemy paratroopers. Four local bridges 'to be defended at all costs'.
Volunteers called for, an old soldier pushed his way to the front with a 'Take me sir, I'll get six of the buggers, one for each of my kids and one for the missus!'
I did.
It was the Court Martial man with the longest ever crime sheet! Still wearing a stripe!

History Repeats Itself

From behind the raised dais, blinding sunshine blazed through the huge end windows of the main hall, directly into the eyes of those seated.

The Senior Course had assembled for the Colonel's 'piece de resistance' – his Final Lecture.

Men who had been exercising found the indoor heat stifling, inducing drowsiness. Overtired with all the night study and operations, eyelids inevitably drooped. Facing the intense light required sustained effort to remain looking alert.

Parading tallest on the right, this was one occasion when the shortest on the left led the way to the front seats – seats fully exposed to the fierce sun. Elsewhere did offer some opportunity of occasionally shifting to seek shadow from the head of the man in front.

By reputation it was to be an extremely boring talk, mostly eulogising Service in the Indian Army. Enthusiasm for a posting to that distant Continent, precisely nil!

The Colonel took it as a personal affront should anybody's eyes close during his discourse. Many, many times in the past he had threatened that the next to so offend would be RTU'd on the spot. Increasingly incensed, rumour had it that this time round he really would carry out the threat. Which had to be taken seriously. Course completed, to be denied a commission, unthinkable! Special effort would have to be made!

With Mother Nature's bewildering ways I had been endowed with one almost blind eye, notwithstanding which so far, somehow, I had managed to 'beat the system'. My own secret. Reading and excessive cramming put me in a vulnerable position.

Blast that window! Why couldn't we have faced the other way?

The Indian Service bit was in full flow.

Why hadn't the man re-vamped his script? All minds rivetted as they were across the Channel and the hoped for success of the landings?

Ten minutes of sheer torture staring ahead, and the sunshine exploded into vivid multi-coloured splashes!

Thump! Something hit my face. Spectacles went flying! Hard-backed covers uppermost, a book lay at my feet!

Sweeping up the missile this was returned to the Colonel; protests of innocence to no avail.

Apoplectically, he was screaming, 'Get Out! GET OUT!'

Decorously, so I was told, one smallish embarrassed figure strode towards the rear door through a sea of faces, some showing open amusement, others looking stunned by this outburst, this tragi-comedy!

Outside, what could one do? Surely not stand there until the end of the lecture? Think! Be positive! But how? All officers were in at that lecture. That is with one exception. The Second-in-Command. Could he be on leave? More likely holding the fort at H.Q. Office. Luckily, he was, and obviously resting.

'Been thrown out by the Colonel, sir, allegedly for being asleep' I explained.

'You weren't?'

'Certainly not sir!'

'Can you tell me what he was on about?'

'But of course, sir.'

He was in a comfortable chair, and motioned me to another.

'Sit down. Now start from the beginning!'

The Colonel's lecture unfolded. The light and the dramatic. All tumbled out, and, not too irreverently, the egotistic claims and theatrical pauses so patently well-rehearsed.

'Splendid!' The 2 i/c pronounced 'You've got it almost word perfect. Heard it so often! Yep, I'll speak to him.'

Expressing gratitude, it was back to await comrades exiting from the hall.

No! There wasn't a chance at all of getting in to explain to the Colonel, and Yes! Unmistakeably, absolutely certainly, it would be R.T.U.!

Generous commiserations were of little consolation. A tormented night followed a miserable evening. What outrageous injustice to be made the scapegoat for all those previous Cadets who'd irritated the Colonel! Ah well! Morning Parade would see an end to the affair. Castigated, humiliated, the worst known!

The final one, it was to be a very special Parade. New barathea dress uniforms, Sam Brownes, would be worn for inspection and approval, followed by a group photograph, and, with announcements of postings, OCTU would be over!

What, for heaven's sake, could be done with one unwanted, and as yet unpaid for, dress uniform?

Prior to the parade, no summons came. Obviously it was to be a thoroughly public dismissal! Strangely, the Parade proceeded. The photograph too. This was ridiculous! Something must be made to happen. But it must be remembered to play it cool and gentlemanly. I would go with decorum and dignity! The War Office would have to be informed. When that happened the right time for explosion, if any! Should it come to it, they could stuff the commission. If my best services not required they could chuck me out of the Army altogether. I would then be able to see to other important duty . . . duty to a hard pressed family for one thing. In such defiant mood I was convinced whatever happened would be for the best.

But what of the Second-in-Command's promise? Had he spoken to the Colonel? I would find out.

In the narrow corridor within HQ Offices a hurrying Colonel ran into me, surprising us both.

'Morning, sir!'

'Morning!' came the response, and from the far end of the corridor, my name.

He well knew why I was there, but not a peep.

The Second-in-Command was more communicative.

'Ah Yes! Of all the Primary, Inters, Seniors in this whole Camp your name's been well and truly bandied about! Colonel wouldn't listen to me! Wouldn't listen to anyone! Until Capt. Day came back from leave late last night.'

Capt. Day, the most senior Training Officer was a key figure responsible for organisation and supervision of Courses at all levels. A big man in all ways. Respected and popular with everyone.

'Capt. Day' he went on, 'challenged the Colonel to name his most successful Staff Officer – the one who'd be most sorely missed! And without even giving the Colonel time to answer offered his immediate resignation if you were chucked out! You can forget the whole thing!'

'Thanks for your help sir! But Capt. Day . . Why should Capt. Day be at all concerned about me . . just another ordinary Cadet?'

'Simple really! Couple of years back he himself was a Cadet here. Sat on the front row. Had a book thrown at him. Threatened with RTU. Accused of being asleep during the Colonel's lecture! Yes, the same one! It hasn't changed a bit!' chuckled the Second-in-Command!

The Cheat

Moss Bros., Hector Powe, and some of their lesser known pretenders did brisk business, each Cadet ordering and being measured-up for service dress uniform and all the necessaries.

The traditional last day of OCTU arrived.

Sartorial inspection, group photograph, formal declaration of commissions and Numbers, and finally, the issue of postings.

It was all over!

Evening declared free, in high spirits, knots of newly made-up one-pippers descended upon Newark to celebrate.

The town was full of troops.

Within minutes someone was frantically shouting and vigorously waving from across the street. Dodging the traffic, in front of us stood a panting Junior Cadet, throwing up an exaggerated salute.

It was Sergeant Hanson!

No longer the terror with three stripes.

'Want you to know how I regret doing what I did! Been on my mind ever since!' he blurted out.

'Not to worry – you did me a dam' good turn!'

'And Crudas gave me a right ol' rollicking!' he added.

'How lucky we were to have such a fine RSM' was all I could think of in answer to that.

'Very lucky, sir.' (How strange to hear that 'sir'.)

'Come and have a drink. We must have a chat!' I pressed.

'Sorry. Can't. Chasing back. Got a Lecture at half-past!'

'Oh! Too bad!' and as we shook hands 'Now don't you *dare* be late on parade!'

Laughingly, he sped off.

How extraordinary! The first ever 'salute' from, of all people, 'The Cheat' who had falsely incriminated we four new Sappers on that opening Parade at Weavers Down, and, the injustice discovered, had been directly responsible for that first-ever, glorious, forty-eight hours leave!

I did really wonder about the *very* long arm of coincidence!

Trapped – on a Landing Craft

Praise the Almighty! I was never a P.O.W.!

The nearest to such terrible experience was to be trapped – incarcerated, on a Landing Craft.

And still further praise! It was not to land on a beach under enemy fire!

Shortly after D-Day a large draft was Continent bound.

Always of course it was forbidden to mention movements of any kind. Equally verboten to carry a personal diary. Sometimes I wish I hadn't been so punctilious over the latter!

Road signposts, railway place names and the like all removed, yet, amusingly, on the South Coast one small corner shop had on show a selection of postcard views, one brazenly emblazoned in large colourful lettering 'NEWHAVEN'. Scribbling a quick 'Love, Bill' this, addressed to my dearest, was slipped into the post.

Our destination was Dieppe.

Wiseacres shook their heads. Exactly as D-Day itself had been imperilled, gale force winds would prevent any crossings in such craft. However, some did nose out.

Ready, we awaited our turn.

Even tied up alongside it was more than just choppy. Men constantly blundered into each other.

Will we sail or won't we? Hours of speculation ended when word came through it had become too risky and sailing abandoned for the day.

Strangely, the expected disembarkation order didn't come.

As daylight began to fade, shouts towards land brought no response. In the gathering darkness, steel floor as mattress, efforts were made to snatch some sleep.

At dawn the weather was unchanged. Hungry, thirsty, surprisingly there was no sign of breakfast! Well, hadn't training included such emergency? From large khaki packs sealed iron rations were extracted, broken open, curiously examined.

Squatting on the floor, small groups formed, endeavouring to boil water on the fiddling ineffectual emergency heating gadget provided. Some were actually successful and a few mugs of revolting char were being passed around, nauseatingly sipped; mostly parted with in disgust. Likewise, the first experimental food remained uneaten. Better go hungry than face a vomiting session!

A further whole night had to be faced!

Hitting the deck all were of one mind.

'Tomorrow we *must* get away!'

But the days and nights came and went. Each a repeat of the past. We were trapped rats!

Hunger forced further experimentations with the foul iron rations, but most made do merely with nibbling at the concentrated cocoa slab.

Somehow, this cursing heap of men maintained morale. Few failed to shave daily. Undrinkable char proved useful for that.

There was now no doubt somebody had boobed! Imagined that all occupied LCP's had left harbour!

Each day no one came anywhere near our assumed empty drifting hulk. Had this been a shipload of animals, and had it been made known, the whole nation would have protested!

Imprisoned in the confines of an LCP by the crass incompetence of our superiors! Repeatedly, the most lewd, painfully lingering death wished upon those responsible!

Amongst this disillusioned, surely unique shipload, anger mounted. Battledress worn day and night became alarmingly creased, bodies smelled; despite adequate ventilation the atmosphere reeked with the stale smoke from countless hundreds of cigarettes.

Unbelievingly, five whole days went by!

When it came, the crossing was a non-event in itself. Remembered only as release.

Arriving in brilliant sunshine, all aboard watched intently as the craft zig-zagged through Dieppe harbour, marvelling at the pilot's skill negotiating huge, house-high, jagged lumps of masonry – parts of the wrecked quays – standing from the water almost as silent monuments to that earlier ill-fated, mainly Canadian frontal attack.

Whenever I see the maple leaf I am reminded.

Reminded of bad-tempered, bedraggled companions' silence in sizing up the audacity, the bravery, of that ghastly raid. Put into context, current hunger and discomforts dismissed as trivia!

Disembarking, the luck of the forgotten craft stayed with it! Unexpected. Not a British uniform in sight.

Hours of waiting, and a couple of lorries turned up, beginning a shuttle service to hastily arranged temporary accommodation at a farmhouse somewhere beyond St. Martin Eglise. The farmyard became a morass of mud with the frequent turnings. The farmhouse, hopelessly inadequate, couldn't cope with the numbers. Earlier arrivals lay spreadeagled occupying all the mucky floorspace.

Men who had not elbowed and shoved their way on to those lorries could but stand around, sandwich in hand, awaiting some miracle of planning.

So! Another cock up!

Sure, this lot would take some sorting out!

Three close pals went into whispered consultation and agreed on a necessary plan of action.

Simple really. A.W.O.L.

Decision made, stepping over mucky bodies, we were quickly outside and heading for the next village.

There, in the central square, various properties were studied. Immediately ruled out, magnificent iron gates and sweeping drive which would almost certainly lead to some stately mansion already occupied by troops. Clusters of small cottages. Terraced houses. A smallish, detached, white-washed, unpretentious property. This, by undiscussed consent, seemed what we were seeking, and worth a try.

One-third of us fluent in French, he knocked on the door. We crossed our fingers! Cautiously, a female opened the door a small way.

'Please! Would it be possible for us to have a wash – well, more of a wash-down?' he ventured.

'Mais certainment! Entrez! Entrez!'

Luck was with us and at first time of asking!

We had actually chosen the Mayor's house, and in no time at all were in friendly and animated conversation with him, his wife, and three young children.

Taking it in turns to bath, the evening was spent delightfully. With totally inadequate thanks, refreshed and in good heart, repeatedly, and most willingly, promising to re-visit, we returned to the filthy farmhouse, to kip down in the back porch, un-noticed and unmissed.

General opinion was to expect a three-day stay. By discreet enquiry it was simple to glean each day's expectations, and just disappear!

A small office-cum-general 'shop' had been set up. How very handy that was! With the purchase of gifts of tinned fruit, and for the children lashings of chocolate bars, each morning it was simple! We disappeared to enjoy our contribution to the Entente Cordiale in exquisite comfort and cleanliness. Can't remember the Mayor's name. Nor the village. But what a beautiful memory of the warmth of welcome, and friendship, of that French home! After five days inexpressively vulgar imprisonment on an LCP it was a glimpse of paradise!

Blue Pencil

Down at the pub, and within the family circle, many a mysterious letter from a loved one in khaki would have been proudly passed around by mums, dads, wives, sweethearts, brothers and sisters.

The letter would bear no clue from whence it came other than an Army post code and the theatre of war.

Much of the contents would have been blue pencilled out. Censored! Proof enough the writer engaged in Highly Secretive Important Operations of the Utmost Magnitude!

Doubtless many letters didn't go through correct channels, but technically all the Company's mail was collected unsealed and handed to the Orderly Officer of the day.

Every serviceman was aware of the need to avoid the folly of letting slip, however trivial, intelligence which might help the enemy. Equally, at home, the campaign 'Careless Talk Costs Lives' was nationally broadcast and well understood.

What would be censored? The OO alone was the arbiter. He probably knew the writer more intimately than the dearest recipient.

In truth, censoring was a tedious, time-consuming, thoroughly boring extra chore though at times highly imaginative scribblings did relieve the tedium, and some 'gems' would lighten the censor's task.

Diaries taboo (not that many would have either the time or inclination to record daily events) his practised eye would fasten on mention of incidents, places, movements, experiences, impressions, and casual news; whether permitted or not, all very often hopelessly missing out on chronology, relevance and fact! The meanderings of a hand unaccustomed to pen and paper frequently defied all understanding!

One casualty of War is that a record of censored material cannot exist! And what an intriguingly hilarious compendium must have been lost to the Nation!

Naming specific Units and placenames of billets were definitely 'out', as was all conjecture on the purpose of a location. These basic indiscretions, easily spotted, blue-pencilled promptly.

It would be the lesser domestic side issues which the average censor would best remember.

Such as the 'opposites' regularly encountered, which so well demonstrated the variability of human nature!

'The grub is O.K./terrible
The War will soon end/will never end.
Everybody is pally/I've no mates at all.
The job suits me fine/is killing me.
Plenty of NAAFI issues/don't get NAAFI rations.
Couple of battledresses/one torn battledress.
Mail comes regularly/your letters don't arrive.
Am fit as a fiddle/am nackered.
Nowt to be afraid of/scared stiff every day.
Get our share of sport/no sport at all.
Local Cafes help/nowhere near any Cafes.
My Sgt. is a great bloke/is a sod.
Weather's been marvellous/still terrible.
Will write every week/no time even to write.
Just had a good shower/can't get a bath.
Had a 24-hr. Pass/no chance of any time off.
Small Co. library/no papers, mags, nothing.
The sick parade daily/no Doctors round here.'

Reading through letters, though probably already known, provided clear barometers of individual morale.

Often it was a temptation to put the record straight; to clarify a blatantly misleading innuendo.

Or simply just to boldly scribble 'LIES!!' Maybe of course this *did* happen. Who knows?

Without very belatedly breaking any Secrets Act, the letter one best remembers was written by the Unit's ace groaner-cum-scrounger.

It went something like this:

'Dear Mum My Own Darling Mum,

> I aynt got any hankies or sox left that big current cake wot you sent was swiped by me mates I didnt get none so send another we never see choclatt or stuff like that Fags I could do with and that watch was pinched All me mates keep saying how much they like those mincepies wot you make the grub is terrible lots of the lads go for beer at a French caff but they got money wot is sent reglar Cant think of any more so God Keep You From Your Loving Son
>
> . . .'

Poor woman!

Those last seven words were underlined in blue pencil . . . HEAVILY!

'Charlie'

Asked to name one or two of the most remarkable characters you ever came across in uniform, perhaps you might like to think a bit.

For me, without hesitation, one would be a Russian.

Yes! A Russian!

His name was Tchapline.

Inevitably, and affectionately, nicknamed "Charlie".

He was born as long ago as 1886 in St. Petersburg now known as Leningrad, into a family of landed gentry with a pedigree stretching back to the thirteenth century.

Volunteering for the Russian Imperial Navy, by 1907 he was commissioned and had started out on a distinguished career.

Early in 1915, when attached to our Royal Navy and commanding submarines manned by British crews, he broke through Germany's blockade of the Southern Baltics to reach the naval base of Kronstadt, for which action the DSC added to his earlier decorations.

On becoming a Lieutenant Commander more honours followed, including Russia's equivalent to the Victoria Cross.

He was then to emerge as Chief of Staff in the defence of the Gulf of Finland, and later, as a Captain, commanded a destroyer squadron.

Quite enough for anyone's lifetime you would think!

But with Revolution about, in collaboration with British, French and Americans, in the guise of a Canadian Colonel he took himself off to Archangel where he successfully organised an Anti-Soviet uprising.

Extraordinarily, he became a British Army major!

When the Revolution became a fait-accompli, in close liaison with Ironside (then a General), he remained on, busily evacuating Archangel and saving many thousands of lives!

An expert linguist, additional to his native Russian he was fluent in English, French and German, with a working knowledge of quite a few mid-European languages.

A brilliant man, and what a career!

Yet he was only 32 years of age, when, as a political refugee, he settled in London.

Twenty years passed.

At the outbreak of the Second World War ('our' war) he would be about 53: still extremely fit and lively.

Although an outstanding sailor, as a gazetted British Army major,

DSO, DSC, MBE, 'Charlie' immediately volunteered.

What happened to his offer of services in 1939 he told me himself.

'No! It's impossible! You're much too old for this War!'

Repeated applications were flatly turned down.

Imagine then the feelings of this outstanding, extraordinary man. Denied an active service role. Unwanted, solely on account of age, by the country of his adoption.

Imagine too, each morning before nine o'clock, a conspicuous solitary figure staging a sit-down incongruously squatting on the steps of the War Office, refusing to take No for an answer!

High ranking Staff officers and civil servants could not avoid him. Whitehall commissionaires remonstrated unsuccessfully.

Such a ritual could not be allowed to go on indefinitely, Charlie was sure of that!

The day arrived, as he explained, somebody called him inside. The exchanges went something like this.

'Look, at your age we can't think about infantry, and that's final! But we might possibly think about letting you have a Pioneer Company'.

'Pioneers? Do they fight?'

'Well, they're armed'.

'They must be able to fight then?' he pressed.

'When they have to. They mostly work'.

'So, they can *fight*. Right! I'll have a Company. Now!' he demanded.

Tchapline, the legendary Tchapline, had his way.

He became a Company O.C. in the Pioneer Corps on which he was very much to leave his mark.

The official history of what is now the Royal Pioneer Corps quotes for example a Corps Commander's report from the Continent dated August 1944:

> 'I found a Pioneer Company under the command of a white-haired Russian which had just proved they were a match for the Germans. On D-Day these Pioneers mopped up a nest of German snipers, coming back with 86 prisoners'.

The Pioneer Company was 120 Company.

It was to be my good fortune, and privilege, to serve that very Company . . . and with Tchapline.

From a Forward Holding Unit at Bourg Leopold, detailed to join him at a place called Mol I had been warned that previously he'd always insisted on vetting and more or less choosing his own officers.

'He'll probably quickly send you packing' they said, 'but tell him you've come purely as a supernumary – sort of temporary!'

Arriving late in the day, having traced Company location to a heavily blitzed clapped out large old property, it was suggested I found and reported direct to the Major.

He wasn't in the shabby ill-furnished room most accurately referred to as the Mess.

Searching for him, wondering what I was in for, opening or attempting to open many doors, room after room was completely wrecked and unuseable. Daylight was failing which didn't help in the darkened passageways.

Believing some kind of noise came from one room I knocked and waited. No reply. Gently opening the door and looking inside it was just another bare empty room. But there, behind the door, sitting in a corner on the floor, out of sight of any interloper, was the Major.

His white head was bent forward. He was listening to a scratchy old record uncertainly revolving on a small very old portable gramophone held between outstretched legs!

The tentative knock hadn't interrupted.

The barely audible record held his attention.

He was completely absorbed.

And tears were streaming down his face!

Silently I closed the door, leaving this already legendary figure to his beloved music . . . and his memories.

So began the most momentous and certainly the happiest period of my own short Service life.

'Charlie', larger than life, was far more than a remarkable character.

He was the perfect O.C. The father and friend to all in his command.

And not surprisingly, every man in the Company would happily have died for him!

Message from the Caravan

A re-union party invitation for all Company officers to meet up with old pals, discovered to be stationed some nine miles away, proved irresistible. Things had been quiet.

As the newest arrival, the most junior, and not known to the pals nine miles away, an offer to stay behind as 'duty dog' was naturally found acceptable.

Left alone, this seemed the signal for things to happen.

A DR screeched to a halt. Wearing three stripes, this of itself unusual.

'Urgent! Will you take me to the Officer in Charge?' he said as I went out to meet him.

'Funny, but that's me!'

The DR Sergeant grinned. He'd noted but one pip!

Absence of all other officers explained, he grinned even more broadly. There was a distinct note of sympathy in his voice.

'Well! Suppose it's OK. Direct from Montgomery!' with which he handed over an envelope boldly stamped 'TOP SECRET. URGENT!'

'Sign here sir, and best o' luck!' he added.

The long field telegram blurringly swam with map references, but clear enough were the key phrases 'enemy paratroops expected', 'defended at all costs', and 'urgent and immediate'.

Of four bridges to be protected, these when identified found to include two of our own Bailey's, one of which completed that day!

Off duty, most men were out in the village for the evening.

Available volunteers mustered, ammo issued, a small party despatched to search for the CSM – all routine stuff – a lorry load streaked out. Not long out of OCTU this was merely putting those 'TEWTS' (Tactical Exercises Without Troops) into practice.

Shatteringly loud and continuous bursts of gunfire suggested we were just too late. Surrounding a wooded area in the prescribed manner quickly revealed, first, an empty parked truck, and then a couple of dozen Canadians, laughingly drunk, blazing away with three or four Bren MG's at a high stack of beer crates.

'Hi there! What are you lot playing at?'

Surprised, the firing ceased abruptly. Almost as quickly one or two recognised the darker khaki of the battledress gifted me by a friendly Canadian Unit.

Mission explained, invited to join us in seeing the first bridge manned, there was a willing rush to oblige! Had any enemy already landed, Hell, they would have been cut to ribbons by quite a formidable slice of armoury!

And so on to secure the other three bridges. All by the book. Men posted for a two-hour stint, with the promise of ample refreshments to come.

Calling at Company headquarters to fix back-up arrangements for the night, it was a little surprising to hear four enemy paratroopers, wearing Canadian uniform, had been picked up. Provided with forged papers and ample pocket money, most extraordinarily they couldn't resist the urge to enter 'our' village cafe to buy some English cigarettes! Presumably to keep them happy from dusk onwards when the bridges were due to be 'dealt with'.

No matter how desperate for a smoke, genuine Canadians wouldn't trespass in this way!

A Sergeant sitting in the cafe had quietly got up and explained this to them. Quite willingly they had admitted to being Germans. Possibly it had occurred to them kamikaze missions best left to the Japs! Pleading in perfect English, they had been allowed to buy the cigarettes!

Major 'Charlie' and the others returned about midnight, and the bridge vigils continued in the normal way.

At first daylight it was a surprise to receive a personal summons to attend Group HQ some few miles distant, there to be faced with a lashing tirade from a furious Colonel.

'Why didn't you bring the telegram here to Group? Who do you think you are making decisions? Why didn't you send your own DR here with it?'

The answer of course was that it hadn't occurred to me.

Returning to Company base, 'Charlie' himself cheerily came out to welcome me back.

'Don't tell me!' he quipped 'you've had a fine old rollicking! Know what you've done? Cheated the old bugger out of putting in for an MC!!'

That hadn't occurred to me either!

The General's Visit

The Rhine immediately ahead, we were up as far as possible, sharing the town's ruins with other forward Supply and Support troops, together with part of the crack Guards Armoured whose tanks laagered in the country-wooded outskirts. Massed infantry were poised just up the road.

A hectic night expected, it was, though without the anticipated serious casualties.

Final preparations were being made for the big push across the river. The enemy doing all possible to prevent it.

At dawn things were much quieter.

During the morning, word came through Command VIP's had set out on a quick spot tour of the Units in the area, hearing which the Major immediately scrapped Daily Orders.

Anticipating how the Guards would be ultra-impressive, determined not to be outdone, he promptly and personally selected and briefed a special 'one-off' Company guard of honour. Picked, smart looking guys, the shortest a six-footer, tallest well over seven feet.

The appointed look-outs spotted the motorcade.

'Fall in the Guard!' screamed the Sarntmajor, himself a splendidly built ramrod six-foot plus and more than capable of screwing out every possible ounce of ceremonial bull.

Inspection by the General and his cavalcade imminent, alongside the massive right marker the Orderly Officer of the day fell in. Fully stretched he might have managed five-foot-four. By comparison the guard looked super giants!

A posse of aides scrambled from cars as The Important Man was being received by 'Charlie' the O.C., well aware this would be a two-minute affair.

In prime position, the dwarfed O.O. was quite uncontrollably grinning all over his face, mirth uncontained at the ludicrous spectacle of which he was the unexpected centrepiece! It was a Bates cartoon in real life! Serious, disciplined composure was impossible! Everybody knew that not an eye should blink. Nobody could fail to miss the comic element. Smiles all round and a buzz of amusement greeted the General. Outrageous!

The General was quick to respond.

First comparing his own height against the lamp-post right marker, he then, with an exaggerated theatrical stoop inspected the diminutive officer.

Mirthful murmurings all round became audible chuckles of delight.

Beamingly, sotto voice, the General addressed the Orderly dog.

'It certainly IS funny! See me later!'

Inspection over, contrived guard dismissed, grinning visitors were persuaded into the Mess, Company officers quizzing how many double whiskies could possibly be sunk were the same welcome extended at all Units to be called at before lunch!

Aloof from the bar, the General and 'Charlie' were in rapid fire conversation.

Soon, however, voices were raised, calling for the Orderly Officer to report to the General. Possibly the smallest officer in the Army made haste to comply.

'How long have you been commissioned?' asked General Dempsey.

'Matter of a few weeks, Sir!'

'Put your second pip up!'

With which the General shot off, his entourage scrambling to keep up with him. The waiting staff cars speeded away. It had all happened so quickly. Not even time for a deferential word of thanks!

Without delay the O.O. tackled Tchapline.

'I know this is your doing Major, but how come I've been given a second pip?'

'Shall we just say for cheerfulness at ALL times? And I'll bet those Guards won't get any promotion in the field for THAT!' chirruped the Major.

'Thanks sincerely, Major, but sorry I upset . . .'

The apology was unfinished. He had gone.

Something somewhat unique followed.

'Charlie' returned, brandishing a couple of pips, needle and cotton, taken from his own kit.

With celebratory drinks all round, one battle dress tunic was ordered to be removed. Protests dismissed, this man, this legendary character, himself set about stitching on those extra pips.

Such is the humility of the truly great!

On the following day Infantry made that very historic push across the Rhine.

For some incident I was despatched to promptly locate the Major. In his own inimitable way he could be anywhere. Way across the fields, in the far distance, there he was, seemingly remonstrating with a German farmworker alongside a pony and trap. Beginning to move, slowly this strange procession advanced. It was some time before it came within hearing distance.

The cart proved to be stacked high with discarded, brand new, rolled up British coats which he personally had retrieved from trenches vacated. 'See this lot?' he had shouted on approaching 'Come and have a look!'

The invitation had been refused. Positively!

'Useful for our Stores!' he grunted on reaching me.

But my finger was still wagging admonishment. I had, with much concern, been gesticulating at the hordes of signs everywhere around.

Large, unmistakeable Warning signs in German and English.

'Danger! Minefield!' . . . 'Danger! Schumines!'

'Tell you what! I'm going to have that second pip stripped off you for disobeying an order!' he chuckled.

Loot

Officially, looting was forbidden.

Many, however, are the confidential stories of those who choose to talk. Particularly in their cups!

Certainly forward Supply and Support troops had ample temptation. Most men found it simple not to bother: had no yen to add to gear which had to be lumped around regularly: nor the time to digress.

Acquisition of such extra weight had to be most carefully eschewed – cameras most common.

If marks were to be awarded for cunning, high on the list would be one Sergeant. An excellent Sergeant (he might possibly glimpse this!). Something of a loner, in off-duty hours he would slip away, solo.

Back home throughout the War it was nigh on impossible to get a watch repaired there being almost a complete dearth of watch springs.

Amongst acres of wrecked buildings he'd discovered a treasure trove! What was left of a Spring manufacturing Works! Small packets which would have neatly rested in his kit bag contained myriads of these tiny springs which netted a tidy fortune on his first UK privilege leave!

It wouldn't surprise if somebody now living in an attractive des. res., comfortably off, might have similarly stumbled upon quite a different treasure!

The cheekiest, most blatant, piece of looting was perhaps the crating and shipping home by one individual of a car in perfect working order.

Not being materially-minded or acquisitive by nature, nevertheless it must be confessed one did not emerge whiter than white (and that washing-power connotation is perhaps quite apt!).

As a token for something or other, pressed into my possession were a couple of expensive white silk shirts which travelled extensively. After the war thousands of miles to Africa; only to be stolen by a Masai tribe servant-boy within an hour's arrival at the Pioneer Depot!

Now, far distanced from those turbulent times, I can quite clearly hear present dear good East Anglian friends pronouncing on the final fate of those pristinely new white silk shirts . . .

'And poetic justice THAT be too!!'

Over-Paid, Over-Sexed, Over-'Ere

During those depressing years of civilian low food rations, black-out and bombing raids, it was not uncommon to hear it.

'Over-paid, Over-sexed, Over-'ere!'

No marks for identifying the doubtful accolade awarded the Yanks.

Things were not helped when Eisenhower was appointed Supreme Commander-in-Chief, Montgomery Second in Command.

The Yanks were tops! The British, second.

There were ceaseless reminders of this. Which was a great pity.

Normally, the individual GI, smartly attired in barathea, collar and tie, was acceptable, friendly, polite, and at pains not to embarrass his less fortunate opposite number, the not so glamorously clad buttoned-up-to-the-neck-in-rough-khaki British Private.

But put the same GI in a crowd amongst his fellows, for some strange reason the good manners, the reasonableness, the charm, all so often seemed to disappear!

Uncle Sam promised the mighty industrial power of the States would be harnessed. The Greatest Nation on Earth would provide armaments, ships, aircraft. Soon, the all-conquering Nazi hordes would be routed and the War won.

Everywhere in Britain the might of the dollar became evident.

Uncle Sam cast his GI in the hero's role, worthy of a star's high pay.

By comparison, the British Private, 'a bit player', with a miserable AB64 Record & Paybook in his pocket, and not much else, very much the poor relation!

Completely different lifestyles!

War is horrible, bestial, dirty and a hell of a lot more which cannot be put into words.

British service life was generally tolerable mainly because it was felt we were all in it together, sharing the same problems, hardships and discomforts.

Most difficulties were of financial origin.

Pay Day a complete mockery!

The average ranker could stomach deprivations yet still contrive to send a pittance home to help loved-ones. To make this possible, self-denial was the norm . . . and accepted.

Now the Yanks were around, comparisons odious!

The pay disparity cut deep.

Penny-pinching hurt more than ever!

Rankers had been through the nightmare of Dunkirk. Seen Britain stand alone against Nazism. Suffered the traumas of families blitzed nightly by Goering's heavy bombers. Been denied leave to help in re-housing. Sometimes being denied leave to attend funerals.

Brash Yanks knew nothing of this!

With them, we were jointly to fight a common War – on grossly unequal terms.

Of course it wasn't surprising there was bitterness.

Strained relationships were unhelped by news of girlfriends, and wives, falling for the free-spending Yank.

With Second Army Troops on the Continental run British and Americans quartered in close proximity moved around over the same territory.

Some misunderstandings were inevitable.

Imagine if you will a Belgian Cafe frequented by a British Unit . . .

Tommies, free for the evening, relaxing over a beer which might, perforce, be the only one and have to last until closing time.

Madame, fussing around, chatting, making 'her boys' as cheerful as she could. She had lived through the German occupation. The British her special friends, 'her boys' represented all Britain stood for in those dark days. Hope. Freedom. 'Her boys' *were* the Liberators! They hadn't much to spend she well knew. At times it was hardly worth her while opening but she regarded her establishment as a sort of Troops Club and would stay open even if but one or two came in during the whole day.

Now then, joining the Tommies, enter two of their own junior officers to discreetly occupy a far corner table, and let it be said, equally limited in the amount of spending power. Pleasantries similarly exchanged, drinks served, Madame back again circulating the main tables, continuing her cheerful banter.

In ones and twos further Tommies arrive to join comrades. Maybe now about a dozen seated, all from the same Unit. Not wishing to inhibit, the two officers drain glasses and prepare to go.

A screaming of brakes, slamming of vehicle doors, loud shouting, and a handful of GI's burst in.

This was the advance party. Pausing to size up occupants of the Cafe, more shouting, urging others to come inside.

Such intrusion defied unwritten rules. Each army used only those Cafes it had 'taken over'. This was tacit and observed wherever the Allies were quartered.

The first Yanks were now ordering at the bar, demanding Madame's haste, others noisily taunting. 'We can take care of this lousy lot!'

Maybe some twenty already half-tight GI's now gathered around the bar, defiantly clamouring for liquor.

Aggression was very much in the air!

Some voices switched to French, which ignorant British wouldn't understand.

'Le premier personnage du mond, Le President des Etats-Unis!' could not however escape anyone's understanding, its very tone recognised as uncomplimentary.

Emboldened by the fact they were taller, mostly of heavier physique and considerably outnumbered those seated, the French faction laughingly exchanged ideas on the next jibe in that language, this, when it came, easily translatable – implying they had been sent over to help out the useless Brits, who were scum.

As 'the French' appeared not to provoke, this was abandoned. Assisted by the topping up of hard spirit, insults were now being hurled around in their own accented English.

Two officers, departure delayed, diplomatically nodded a good-night. The result of this confrontation would become known on the morrow.

Early morning full Company Inspection.

O.C. together with Orderly Officer for the day going through the usual procedure, looking each man up and down whilst strolling through the ranks.

On this occasion obliged to stop in astonishment facing a man with freshly mutilated face, cheek bones showing through.

'Good God! What's happened to you Ellison?'

'Ran into a door Sir' the response.

Further along, another, sporting a huge black eye.

'Football Sir. Somebody's elbow, Sir'.

And another with bloodied face.

'Tripped over in the dark Sir!'

So it went on.

Men with forage caps set at impossible angles in unsuccessful attempts to conceal split scalps and cauliflower ears. A few with makeshift bandages. Others speckled with plaster strips. Fingernail inspection, that always random affair, revealed bleeding hands, knuckles shorn of skin.

Exchanging a flutter of a wink to his OO the Major loudly let it be known that he wouldn't stand this horseplay of men fighting amongst themselves. Not in *his* Company!

By now the Orderly officer had mentally accounted for the dozen he'd left in the Cafe.

Stopping at one, desperately looking fixedly ahead through almost fully closed eyes, he whispered a concerned enquiry.

'How did you get on?'

Pin-sized eyes twinkled back. From excessively red and almost toothless gums, with obvious difficulty but undisguised triumph came the confidential response.

'Chucked 'em all out, sir!'

'But there were twice as many!'

'Took us an hour, sir!'

Parade dismissed, twelve men were officially being escorted to the three-tonner and on to the M.O. known to be in the next town. To make absolutely sure an M.O. was found, the Orderly Officer joined the driver.

Apart from the obvious, dislocated shoulders and damaged limbs were diagnosed, given first aid treatment and dressings. A couple more seriously injured with head wounds would have to be sent on somewhere for further examination.

Anyone spotting the lorry on its return trip might have imagined it subbing as an ambulance. Though surely, no such transport could be running around with a male voice choir aboard?

It was the first, and the last, *compulsory* Sick muster in the experience of that young officer who happened to Orderly Dog that day! He could *not* condone bar brawls, but this lot, to a man, had turned out and paraded almost as though nothing had happened! They had been provoked, heavily outnumbered, horribly mauled, yet steadfastly refused to report 'sick'.

Right or wrong, these were 'his' men!

In his heart he knew that if and when the time came for legitimate fighting he wouldn't exchange them for the crackest of crack troops. They call it esprit-de-corps. A bond. A trust. An understanding. Respect and honest friendship for each other which transcends rank. (Incidentally events were to prove his heart had dictated correctly).

To this day however, recalling that Belgian Cafe rough-house, he can't resist a little personal smile should someone trot out that wartime catchphrase 'Over-paid, Over-sexed and Over-'ere'!

Antwerp

Few would give thought to, or pretend any knowledge of grand strategy, but it was obvious to all that the taking of Antwerp was important. It was simple to understand that for best military advantage the Port, which had suffered surprisingly little, would need to become fully operational as speedily as possible.

The city was bursting at its seams with troops. Many Units just hung around waiting for instructions.

For something to do, the Rex Cinema which operated almost non-stop, was naturally most popular and always full.

It had a direct hit. Mass carnage!

Passing at the time, a couple of our own Company's Sergeants assumed overall rescue directions, diving in, getting panic under control and generally directing rescue operations. Witnessed by so many, some time later they were actually 'Commended'!

Quite recently this tragic incident somehow cropped up in conversation, since when a local acquaintance, on meeting, never fails with the greeting 'Ah! The man whose comrades saved my life!' Trapped, he had given up all hope of being extricated. Suffering terrible damages, a wreck, had been invalided out of the Forces.

'Commended!' he invariably snorts 'Those Pioneer sergeants ought to have got bloody VC's!!'

It was not only the last of the cinema. Monty promptly slapped a ban on all public gatherings.

Ships were hastily being directed into the Docks.

On fine days the trails of V2's streaking from Holland towards England could clearly be seen, the intensity noticeably increasing. On dull, misty days - we quickly tumbled to this - both V1's and V2's would be switched to fall on Antwerp. Troops became 'bomb-happy', with barrages completely ignored unless the ground opened up uncomfortably near. The job in hand was too important to bother with interruptions. Pioneers and Canadians laid many miles of rail line in the Marshalling Yard. *This* was the target the Germans were hellbent on stopping.

For each Unit, daily 'targets' of a particular distance of line would be set. When achieved it was 'down tools' and away back to billets; which created real interest, incentive and rivalry. There was no doubt that English, Scots, Welsh, Irish and Canadian 'miles' differed alarmingly! Whatever their interpretations of land measure however, the Sergeants (bless 'em all!) made sure each squad pulled its weight for the benefit of the whole. The system was hugely successful.

Poor old Belgium was going through yet another crisis. Van Acker replaced Pierlot as Premier. Dockworkers demanding higher danger pay, for ever holding meetings, threatened to stop work. Negotiations broke down, and strike they did!

Military construction work came to a halt.

Personnel from all Units and Corps moved in, responding to the exhortation to keep the ships, cranes and lorries turning round. The Port did not grind to a standstill as forecast by the dockers – who stood in their hundreds at the gates, aghast at the vast number of loads streaming out.

This seemed fine, but in all truth, within the Docks it was muddle, hopeless confusion and a complete lack of organisation! Approached to organise some co-ordination the most senior officer 'didn't want to know', insisting his instruction was to concentrate on, and clear, just the one specific ship.

Pioneers assumed overall management!

Pioneers always seemed to have somebody with the right experience and ability, whatever the challenge. Foul-ups and bottle-necks were gradually sorted out. VIP's breezing in were directed to wholly unofficial operational headquarters, to be gleefully driving away within minutes to locate more transport and drivers 'to satisfy the demands of that little chap in Shed 7'! Schweik had dreamt he'd handled all this palaver before!

Something quite new however popped up later.

From a railway bridge vantage point it was apparent an evening outgoing train had slowed to walking pace. Dropside doors of trucks were noisily banging open, and large crates dropping out! Troops, not British, emerging from bushes on both sides of the goods train raced down embankments to grab and drag the booty to waiting lorries.

'Give us the tools and we'll finish the job!'

At home, Churchill's message had gone to factories, with enormous response!

Those crates, though for the front, did not contain armaments, but NAAFI brandy and whisky!

Schweik consulted as to what should rightly be done.

The official reply 'Nothing! You didn't see anything! Forget it!', reasoning being that ensuing inter-Armies trouble would eclipse the crime itself. And what good advice that was! Without Schweik's help higher authority was tackling crime in Antwerp.

One particular counterplan may not appear in any War Diary. Montgomery personally chose the day for a swoop. In the strictest confidentiality (O.C.'s and 2 i/c's only) each Unit received two tickets. Any movement in the town that day would be limited to the holders of those passes.

What a haul the day brought! Deserters galore! All wearing normal battledress. One whole 'Unit' if you please actually masquerading as Military Police, complete with 'official' Detachment Number, flashes, full transport, full official documentation, complete with huge notice board outside splendid Headquarters! The whole gamut! Even to the correct number of officers, NCO's and other ranks (one of our own AWOL rascals included!). Antwerp that day was full of very surprised, very red, faces! Somebody in Intelligence, deservedly, can take a bow!

About this time too, Monty's popularity was further enhanced when, war or no war, the thrill of Home Privilege Leave was introduced.

On the broad front steps of Capellen House the names of those who 'qualified' went into the hat and the first batch drawn for. It was one very rare occasion when the permanently excused eagerly went on parade! Such a full assembly just had to be marked in some special way. The Company had never had a religious service; it was time for rejoicing, time to Thank God! Observed with the most uncanny reverence, it was generally agreed as fitting, giving those who wouldn't go anywhere near a church, the opportunity of offering up a silent 'good luck for leave' prayer!

The Major's long service qualified him to go with the first draft. He would be away fourteen days.

Robbed of key figures and under strength isn't it remarkable how often an outfit runs into problems and difficulties?

Stationed in such a large place as Antwerp, incidents can be related and remain in sharp focus much more readily compared with events in the many unknown and remote hamlets. Though, without doubt, the suddenness of total and ultimate responsibility helps too!

Firstly, a real crisis! The precious main railway line was breached. Catastrophic, Second Army HQ would have been notified. The CO of RE Railway Construction Groups had alerted senior Sapper specialists. At the scene, word went out for all heavy equipment within the area to be brought in. There was none!

Desperately vital, the job would have to be done entirely by hand! A whole Pioneer Company would be required. And of all Pioneer Companies available, the one sans its OC detailed!

The crater was huge. High built up ground had disappeared. It was a freezing night's work carried out in primitive fashion just as the ancient Egyptians would have done it, which is why the massive repair became known as Operation Sphynx!

Secondly, returning from the Docks to quarters the whole Company watched a V2 blow a sister-Company's billets to smithereens! In the ghastly shambles, ignoring falling bricks, timber and other hazards, everyone, to a man, struggled unceasingly, pulling out survivors. Men known to us. Doing what we could for the injured. Carrying away the dead. A sad, and sickening experience!

And thirdly, another kind of disaster, but not wholly of the enemy's making. A detachment of fifty or so based in a town some nine miles distant had kipped down for the night. The building went up in flames, spreading to adjoining civilian properties.

Like the lone Selkirk horseman who galloped back from Culloden with the sad news, somebody, somehow, covered the nine miles into Company HQ. Quickly dressing, a small party chased over to discover the officer in charge of the detachment not at the scene. Conflagration eventually contained, crowd dispersed, troops and civilians accommodated elsewhere, attention switched to locating the missing officer.

A tipoff obtained at his official personal quarters, an address about a mile away was stormed. He was hauled out of bed with a mistress. Both naked! We weren't in the mood to hang about! Allowing for collection of his clothes he was directed to the utility van as he was. Starkers! Nothing to the later dereliction-of-duty shock!

No! Antwerp was not a favourite stop!

As I said, it was bulging with troops.

Not all could be expected to come anywhere near Monty's high expectations.

He himself was probably just as glad to leave the place behind!

Field Cashiers

Reaching Germany, a conglomeration of Belgian, Dutch, French and German coinage in the pockets of hard up soldiery, Deutschmarks would become the only legal tender.

'Units will make arrangements to exchange with the nearest Field Cashiers'. How easy to issue Orders!

Second Echelon staff comfortably ensconced at Base appeared to have little idea of life in Germany – sheltering in clapped-out desolation: uncertainties of each day: meeting pre-determined tasks in crude conditions. Units more than fully stretched, transport likewise; this money business one more hassle!

All ranks assembled, here was a Pay Day in reverse! Paying in one's total wealth, and signing for it!

To comply, a suitably columnised master list of some two hundred and fifty names had been prepared on which to record detailed amounts of separate currencies received from each man.

Coins and notes of each currency totted up, these then reconciled with figures accumulated on the master list. By the religiously dim light of a tilly lamp, individual coinage had been bagged and tagged.

A painstaking long night's work interrupted only by a low level bombing sortie rousing everybody and bringing the consolation of the ever-refreshing char!

The job continued, transposing into Deutschmarks the amount each individual would expect, and revealing the full wealth of the whole Company. Horizontal and vertical castings re-checked, the tedious business was over. What a slog! All was ready for a prompt exchange and a quick pay-out. Nobody was likely to be happy until correct cash safely back in pocket!

Essential morning duties over, spondulics stacked in the utility van, an always-dedicated driver together with a bleary-eyed Second-in-Command-cum-erstwhile-financier set off to comply with that delightfully naive instruction 'Exchange with nearest Field Cashiers'. Nearest? Hell! Where were ANY?

Blindly touring, it was a guessing game! Many suggestions tested, mileage ticking up, valuable time flying, eventually, to unbounded joy and relief, there it was! A small roughly arrowed sign 'Field Cashier' pointing through a hedge into a field. But goodness knows how long this business would take: how many Units would be on the same mission. Daylight was limited. After queuing at least we would have plotted a direct route back to Company HQ . . . Then the pay-out would have to be immediate. God! It was going to be another very long, long day!

Surprise! Surprise! Not a queue in sight! Our luck was in! In solitary isolation stood one small trailer-caravan with a dropdown serving hatch.

Ferried from utility to caravan, armfuls of bagged money were lumped in national heaps, contents and numbers of bags fastidiously declared. Grand number of bags announced, two purposeful arms inside the caravan swept the whole lot with a tremendous crash to the floor!

'Hey! What are you playing at?' gasped the startled 2 i/c.

'How much do you want?' the casual reply.

'What! You're not going to check!'

'Nope!'

The full required amount of Deutschmarks, and in the requested values, were tossed on to the counter.

The whole thing had taken but three minutes!

Brandishing his master list, splutteringly cursing a whole night's toil, an unbelieving 2 i/c demanded explanation.

'Trouble was most Infantry mobs chucked in loads of unsorted cash. Couldn't sort that lot out!'

'But how would you know the exchange total correct?'

'Don't! They reckon we should have gone into each Unit and done the work'.

'Maybe they're right, but why didn't Base think so?'

'Because we just haven't got the blokes up here, and they know it!'

'So anyone who finds he can't properly refund can come back for more?'

'Well . . . er . . . Sure!'

'And some slap-happy types could get away with a massive rip-off?'

'Maybe! Quite likely!'

Some strange things certainly happened in Germany!

How could those trailer-loads possibly be reconciled?

And where did all the vast collection of filthy lucre finish up?

One wonders if anything of this massive financial operation appears anywhere in any Official Diary.

Know any wealthy gentlemen-farmers round your way who might have helped out a harrassed Pay Corps?

Rheine Wine

Rheine had been appallingly knocked about.

The acting Town Major visited, he repeated the request.

'Accommodation for a whole Company?'

'Yup! Two hundred and forty. Plus five officers'.

'Not a chance!'

'But there must be . . . got to be . . . somewhere!'

Unenthusiastically, he scanned a wall map of the town.

'There's just . . .' he started.

'Yes, go on, just what?'

'One possibility. Haven't breathed a word about it.'

'About what?'

'One large clapped-out house'.

'With a roof?'

'Mostly. But it's the cellars'.

'Cellars? What's wrong with the cellars?'

'Full of wines and spirits!'

'Infantry missed it?'

'Went right through!'

'And you're worried?'

'Right! Of course!'

'You can trust me! . . . Now where is it?'

Opening the drawer of a table serving as a desk he pulled out and tossed across a massive bunch of labelled keys.

'Quick look-see and I'll be back!'

A superficial recce was enough.

The whole structure appeared sound, staircases negotiable, upper floors usable. Blasted windows appeared the only real damage.

Within minutes it was back to the Town Major.

'Thanks! Booked! I promise you won't regret!'

Local enquiry confirmed the house indeed belonged to the largest Wine & Spirit wholesaler in the whole area. He had fled, with his family. The cellars, those amazing cellars, thoroughly explained the Town Major's reluctance and nervousness!

As arranged, the whole Company moved up the following day.

Priorities over, the OC and Sergeant-Major couldn't wait to go underground!

Opening each locked door produced gasps of utter disbelief! On every wall, from floor to ceiling, wide shelves packed tight with bottles! Dusty, undamaged, undisturbed!

We'd struck gold!

A prize of war which would compensate in small part for all the grim and unpleasant!

Even as the inspection proceeded a strategy was being devised. Over-riding all, assurances given to the Town Major would be strictly honoured!

Sergeants would be briefed and charged on trust with personal responsibility for every man in each squad.

After 1900-hours each evening, by a rota to be arranged, all would individually select one bottle for personal consumption. Strict check would be kept on returned empties!

And any abuse of the privilege, in any way at all, the cellars would be immediately locked. Permanently!

This Company had been outstandingly successful. None better shod, clothed, fed; nor had mail and NAAFI rations more regularly. Knowing this, in the squalor of atrocious conditions, and whatever the danger, men had responded with total commitment, sure in the knowledge each man was respected, with dignity.

In short, it was a happy Company.

It is often said, and rightly so, Sergeants are the backbone of the Army. Those Sergeants kept a firm grip on this liquor bonanza!

Cheerful faces on morning parades gave no hint of hangovers! On the contrary, the unprescribed medicine added fresh sparkle! The Sick parade non-existent!

Of course no-one could possibly be naive enough to imagine that somehow the inventive, flexible Pioneer hadn't creatively used his good fortune! Popularity amongst civilians around gave this some firm credance!

Top Brass would have swooned to hear of the exclusive Rheine Night Club, its Constitution and unwritten rules of membership!

The whole secret was faithfully honoured.

Not a man stepped out of line!

Remarkably, other troops quartered in the town remained in ignorance of those richly stocked cellars.

There was but one visitor.

The Town Major.

A welcome and regular drinking companion: a most relieved man, constantly expressing astonishment. And gratitude!

• • •

Within days of moving into Rheine a four-paged closely-typed document arrived from Base Headquarters.

Foolscap size; so it was noted!

Headed boldly 'VERY IMPORTANT': outlining likely problems Units would find having reached Germany, suggesting various ways of enhancing morale, the importance of making extra effort in the interests of men's welfare, stressing the value of regular mail and NAAFI collection, and so on.

It gave us a laugh!

The Company Clerk, observing Nil Returns were required (the usual format on all Base directives), described a large red '0' on the front page, and for some strange reason returned the whole document to Base.

Some days later the Major was summoned to Group Headquarters and in real trouble!

He could offer no explanation to an enraged Group Colonel – for onward transmission to Base – how a *second* similar large red '0' had been added, in parallel, to the document's face!

Neither could Company Office personnel suggest any explanation!

We did agree however the Rheine wine might possibly have had something to do with it!

Red Blanket

In yet another flattened town centre it seemed no property remained whole.

To make way for military traffic a narrow channel had been bulldozed along the line of what would have been the main street, leaving rubble house high.

Locals remaining, women, children, older men were huddled in communes in the lesser damaged outskirts.

Within the ravaged town the occasional signboard indicated some Units had already established quarters of sorts.

A quick tour searching for roof cover resulted in settling on one area, grotesque nevertheless, as the only likely prospect. It would have been a street of terraced property, one broken end wall carrying the remains in German of the now familiar white-lettered exhortation to fight for Hitler to the last man.

It was no time for being choosey!

Staking our claim with the erection of our own Company sign, the small advance party immediately set to work.

'Keep Out' warnings boldly chalked up on the more dangerous fabrics, a debris of bricks, timber, mutilated furniuture and domestic riff-raff was hastily hurled clear of the more promising cover. Stopping to make rough assessments as to the number of men each cleared room would take, then tackling any accessible upper floors. More checking, doubling back ascertaining, guessing, on all possible kipping-down space, until agreeing a complete Company might perhaps be directed to immediate, if somewhat risky, temporary cover. Toiling to dark, exhausted, the small advance party, endeavouring to ignore the nauseating stench, settled down; with dawn resuming work with intensified urgency.

By mid-day the Company had been ferried up along damaged, battle-strewn roads. A long wearisome journey! A journey which brought no rest! The first priority of all men was to finish clearing out and attempt to clean, those quarters to which we were now committed.

Jettisoned rubbish accumulated. Many bonfires sent thick, choking, acrid black smoke belching around, which, at least, offered contrast to the all-pervading stink.

Snatching mugs of tea, the filthy work proceeded non-stop. By nightfall, the full complement prepared to kip down, reasonably sheltered. This was much better than erecting tentage somewhere out of town. Even in warmer weather we'd had enough of that!

It was now freezing! Teetering window frames having been knocked out, apertures open to the elements promised a chilly night.

Urgent and serious warnings had been issued. Surrounding blitzed remains strictly out of bounds. No exploring for loot! A disease hazard, the obvious red blankets in the wreckage quite definitely taboo!

The enemy had favoured us with a reasonably quiet day. May the night continue so! In arctic conditions the Company settled down.

As ever, in whatever circumstances, customary final rituals followed.

Cheery words with those on first guard and a tour of inspection.

Orderly Officer and Sergeant-Major agreed though it had been a long hard grind, and despite the mess, the moving in operation had gone quite well. Pity the men had to be so scattered about, but it was good to see them bedded down. Carefully the two scrambled over debris, picking their way from one lot of men to another, exchanging comments in whispers, not wishing to disturb.

Suddenly the night's stillness was pierced by a choking, paralysed shriek from the officer!

He had spotted a German red blanket!

Unbelievable! Here in a room which men had so laboriously toiled to cleanse! One bedraggled, filthy, verminous, wholly-against-orders, German red blanket!

Roused from deep sleep, men were rubbing eyes: others, expecting emergency, already sitting up, alert, seeking explanation.

'Sarnt-Major! Put him on a charge!'

The Sergeant-Major strode angrily and very purposefully forward towards the culprit.

From below the offending red blanket not one but two faces appeared.

The Sergeant-Major's voice was ominously quiet and controlled.

'And the charge, Sir? Don't tell me!'

Allen's Club

The whole place was stinking. The stench of death and desolation.

Amongst the rubble, all that remained of a fierce battle, the odd building had been cleared, patched up, and some sort of shelter contrived.

With approaching darkness palliasses thrown down were necessarily at much less than the regulated space apart.

In this now familiar turmoil, forward support troops somehow existed and functioned.

Meeting up with a familiar face from another Unit it was impossible to contemplate the invitation 'When you can, slip over to our place for an hour'. Things were much too uncomfortable to squeeze in any visitors.

Something would have to be done to provide a meeting place, and quickly. Negotiations with NAAFI, pooling off-duty voluntary labour, and a small hall was identified, cleared and made fit for general 'leisure' use.

This achieved, why not an Officer's Club?

Anything makeshift would be more than welcome!

Troops had volunteered to bring about their own den. Officers likewise would have to take their greatcoats off.

The thought was put into action.

A ground floor room of a terraced house was tackled. Extricated from the debris of a corner cafe, chairs and small tables willingly repaired. One or two concentrated on ingeniously fashioning a mock optics display. The preparatory work had attracted interest and help. Word quickly got round. Appeals and publicity unnecessary. Enquiries and scrounging all round and a vast harvest of bottled spirits and beer promptly accumulated. Finally, old Army blankets, crudely nailed up, formed an effective blackout porch.

There would be no opening date or ceremony. A steady trickle of officers popping in to help and this roughly thrown together effort rapidly took on a passable impression of a British pub.

With one difference. All booze was free!

Allen had been the inspiration.

A great hulk of a man, he was in his element playing mine host, exuding bon homie, exchanging banter with all and sundry from an increasingly wide range of Regiments and Corps.

On a brass monkeys night, though a cheerful wood fire blazed merrily, all remained great-coated.

'Charlie', the Major, had promised to drop in by way of inspecting this creation of his junior officers. Impressed, persuaded to stay awhile, he chose a corner seat clear of the inevitable cluster standing at the bar. Laughter, recognitions, introductions, reminiscences, noisily filled the small room.

Rhine crossing imminent, infantry filled the next town. Squadrons of the Guards Armoured were with us and amongst the 'customers'. Officers from all Support Units had crowded in, RASC, RA, REME, and so on; Sappers and Pioneers predominant.

The protective screen of blackout blankets once more being drawn aside, two tall young Guards officers entered, impressive in appearance as would be expected. Strangely, in the terribly filthy and ravaged town of Goch, their greatcoats incongruously pristine, immaculately pressed: not a whisper of ever having been soiled or tightly folded.

Looking around the makeshift Club, notwithstanding the buzz of jollity, cultured voices could not avoid being overheard.

'Rather a rough house, what?'

'Bloody appalling!'

'Couldn't they do better than this?'

In the hush which followed, hackles bristled on the backs of those volunteers who had handled and disposed of indescribable filth to provide the meeting place.

Remarkably, without protest, very courteously, two young one-pippers were invited to name their drink. Glasses filled and handed over, cash offered, it was explained this was no ordinary pub, but truly a 'free' house.

Then it was one of the Guardees saw a shoulder flash!

'Pioneer Corps! Christ! What the hell are *they* doing here?'

It wasn't his flash they'd seen, but the big feller behind the bar reddened and choked.

'Insulting bastard! Apologise immediately!' he demanded.

'Why should I?' came the defiant answer.

Leaning forward, the huge hulk, grabbing the speaker by the lapels, lifted and hurled him into the optics, sending the temporary bar counter crashing over, with chaos and wreckage everywhere! Counter, tables, chairs, bottles, glasses all in a grotesque mess!

It had all happened in seconds. Now the big fellow, kicking his way through the damage was pulling the youngster to his feet.

'I'll show you why your bloody Pioneers are here!' he was shouting.

Dragging the unfortunate guardsman through the melee he was

making for the Major who had remained impassively, quietly, seated, though surrounded by a welter of broken glass and chairs.

'Please! Please Major, do me a favour! Please undo your greatcoat. Please!' he pleaded.

Imperturbably, 'Charlie' resisted.

Again the big fellow appealed, this time supported by voices all round.

'Go on Sir!'

'Open his eyes, Sir!'

'Educational process, Major!'

'Do us all a favour, Major!'

So pressed by the whole gathering, with a wry amused smile 'Charlie' permitted eager hands to undo a button.

The guardees head was being thrust still nearer.

Others jumped in to assist the unbuttoning.

Very quickly the Major's battledress tunic was revealed, displaying lines of ribbon: a mass of colour which Monty himself would not achieve!

'See those? See those?' Allen was barking 'Have a damn good look! That's *Service!* That's why your bloody Pioneers are here!'

Two shocked, bewildered, wholly unpopular guardees, greatcoats now crumpled and bespattered, hastily retrieved caps, glad to be free from the maelstrom, and out into the dark.

At Company HQ the following morning a very distinguished visitor arrived anxious to have a word with the Major. None other than the Guards Commanding Officer. He wished to apologise. To explain the two youngsters had been posted to him almost direct from University. Had only been through initial training having been in the OTC, and had just arrived. Within hours had been recommended to find the makeshift Club. Also, he'd brought some of his officers round ready and prepared to remedy all the havoc immediately.

That wasn't necessary.

Allen had already apologised for his rush of blood and, unknown to anyone, had spent most of the night at work, repairing and restoring.

But that evening, how marvellous it was to see in a crowded, rearranged makeshift Club, a couple of great pals sitting together. The Guards C.O. and 'Charlie'. Like two schoolboys themselves, hilariously swopping stories!

In all fairness too, it should be mentioned both those young Guardees turned up on the succeeding night, each carrying a couple of bottles, and offering to do a stint behind the bar or wash the glasses,

anything to help out – which was bully for them!
'We've heard all about Pioneers!' said one.
'Mighty glad they stuck us in the Guards!' said the other.

• • •

There was a sequel.

Within days the tremendous roar of artillery barrage, continuous throughout the night, presaged the crossing of the Rhine.

Just a few miles away, at Xanten, the operation was held up. Untimely, inconveniently, a mighty big crater appeared in the river bank at the very point where RE stores had been specially accumulated for throwing across a pontoon bridge.

Crack infantry poised to cross, the Corps Commander sent out urgent signals for volunteer work parties to repair the breach. Alas, without response!

Timings critical and immediate action necessary the decision was taken to order a Unit in.

One Pioneer detachment!

Fully exposed to direct withering fire, and with inevitable casualties, under the direction of one Lieutenant. None other than the huge bloke who went berserk at that makeshift Club!

Would he have remained unhonoured? Surely impossible: but in the heat and demands of action much was overlooked.

We heard he survived.

Is Allen now frustratingly sitting about in a wheelchair somewhere: just another Number, Rank and Name?

And by the way I didn't witness that 'job', having been switched to another Company which crossed a few days later.

At the very spot.

Over a pontoon bridge.

At Xanten.

Quietly!

Mein Kampf

The Füehrer himself had not allowed a whisper of such possibility!

Elegant good living had been interrupted by wholly unimagined invasion of the Fatherland!

The owner of the large mansion had retreated, taking his family to another property, in the Harz Mountains.

The comfortable quarters were hardly damaged.

This was luxury!

The Library attracted. What a rich array!

Here was evidence of position. The obligatory show of good taste! In astonishing variety a wealth of marvellously attractive creations of the printers' craft! Heavy tomes. Whole series. A treasure store of gold-leafed edgings, impeccably, expensively, bound. Reference volumes. Travel Guides. Huge, magnificent portfolios of 'Beautiful Germany' packed with panoramic photographs of stunning beauty.

At eye level, occupying the most prominent position, an ornate hardback copy of Hitler's 'Mein Kampf' in mint condition – not even, as with so many other books, carrying a flourished signature inside. Thumbing through the pages some stuck together. Quite obviously it had remained unopened: which would not have amused the author!

Alongside this, so many publications glorifying Nazism! The absent owner, good businessman, clearly knew what he was about. Good Party show. Pure and prudent exhibitionism!

Children's books too, which appeared pristine. One, a small slim, delightfully colour illustrated 'In Happy Summertime All Children Go To Play'. In more normal times when browsing through some bookshop back home just the thing as a present for the babe!

It was posted off to one very young son, Sandy – 'Souvenir from Germany' scribbled on its flyleaf. Those beautifully painted pictures would entrance, and the so strange German script intrigue!

As an afterthought and a reminder of that lavish library, the glaringly unwanted exhibition piece of 'Mein Kampf'' also became a personal memento.

Somewhere, perhaps up in the loft, it's still around. I too haven't ever bothered to open it!

'Ich Liebe Dich'

Neatness and tidiness exuded.

The small end-terraced house scrupulously clean.

It positively sparkled!

Houseproud fraus had descended on it: swarmed through every room. All thoroughly spring-cleaned within the last twenty-four hours.

Contents appeared to be unchanged. Tables, chairs, carpets, crockery, photographs, books, pictures, seemingly all left in accustomed position.

This was no show-off house. Far, far more! It was a cherished home. Modest property perhaps, but a lovingly-tended home!

The comfortable little bedroom, its colour scheme, the trinkets, had a decidedly feminine touch.

An attractive flower-patterned counterpane covered the single bed. Now washed, immaculately ironed, and whiter than it had been for a very long time, my own bedroll sheet with its inbuilt pillowcase cover was in place.

The whole atmosphere suggested this room belonged to a young, single fraulein. Without consciously thinking of it at the time there was no evidence of a child having been accommodated in the house. No toys.

On the walls of the bedroom, photographs were evidently of family content. By the bed, one of a serious, good-looking young man in open-neck shirt. Undoubtedly a substitute. The normal would have shown him proudly in uniform. Wehrmacht perhaps, or Air Force, possibly Stormtrooper. A change clearly made in order not to offend.

Neatly tied with pink ribbon, bundles of letters were stacked in the open top compartment of the bedside table, which, together with the floral lampshade and the single photograph formed the focal point. Almost a shrine.

By the street door, just off a small lobby, the ground floor room on the left had been converted into a bed-sit: this for a batman. Though very much trusted, in pain of mortal consequence he accepted the advice No Looting, No Visitors!

Wakening me with the usual cheering morning cup of char he bubbled volubly on, enthusing over the spotless well-ordered kitchen, the over-supplied amount of utensils; marvelling at the happy turn in our luck!

Breakfasting in unusual isolation, it was soon time to leave the new luxury; to rejoin the hundred or so men billetted across the street.

This accommodation, this Officer's Mess, was not a personal choice.

The detachment occupied a village infant school. The head teacher quickly and most gratefully had noted the concern and kindness shown by British troops to the half-starved ill-looking children. The District Nurse too expressed delight; the school her chosen centre.

Unknown at the time, it was approaching V.E. Day.

Almost half the Company was on location assisting a platoon of Royal Engineers in the reconstruction of a demolished main line railway bridge over the Ems near Essen. Work under way, top brass, British and American, had inspected. Conducted to the living quarters, the school's office-cum-stockroom occupied by the officer had displeased. To provide somewhere away from the men where VIP's could meet, and chat, a proper Officer's Mess must be set up. A house would be commandeered immediately!

Explained to the village fraus, this, without any pressure, would be left entirely to them.

Promptly, the end terraced house had been vacated. When ready for official handing over a group of women waited anxiously around. 'Wunderbar' pronounced, they had clapped and happily dispersed.

As a routine, throughout the day two or three cooks, together with the batman, remained on guard. Yes! Of course! If it pleased them the fraus could be allowed into the house to keep it spick and span!

The ready availability of tinned food must have made cooks and batman more than popular! All in all the whole detachment was made to feel genuinely welcome, everlastingly hearing how thankful all villagers were that the feared 'Ruskies' had not moved in!

Retiring on the second night in the commandeered new quarters, somewhat guiltily I reached for one of the brightly ribboned bundles crammed into the bedside table. Skimming quickly through some of the epistles, they were, as expected, in the same handwriting.

Passionate love letters!

Re-tying the bundle exactly as found this was carefully replaced into its original position.

Each following night, interestedly, compulsively, the same performance was repeated. The same furtive perusal of German script: each letter, each bundle, restored in correct order.

By fortune of War I was an intruder.

Conscience dictated I was also prying into a very, very, personal and intimate relationship.

But why had this young girl left her most dearest possessions there? And so prominently?

To identify with another serving soldier? Someone who himself would have written many similar letters? Someone who would *understand?*

Knowledge of the German language limited, nevertheless the written word did enable the general context to be understood. A picture spanning a number of years unfolded. All the customary heartbreaks of the parted. Repeated assurances of fidelity. The full range of endearments and hopes for the future which could be written in any language.

Here was a young man sincerely and hopelessly in love, desperately striving to convey his feelings in writing! In this War many millions of such letters must have been penned! Mail, the one tangible connection!

Truth to tell though, I was looking beyond those oft-repeated expressions of love and faithfulness. Searching, almost clinically, for a special letter. The one containing news of Leave . . . 'Coming home . . . to see you . . . to be in your arms . . . next month! . . . next week! . . . Morgen!' The search unsuccessful.

Switched from one front to another, this young man did not appear to have had any leave whatsoever!

Unless POW or with SEAC in some far-flung part of the globe we British didn't do too badly for leave!

I wondered.

Had I stumbled on the one main weak link in that once powerful all-conquering German Army? The one reason perhaps why I was where I was, reading those intensely intimate letters?

A senior American had put it to me that the average country folk around 'were the salt of the earth – just like our own way back home'. He was right of course. But they could not escape responsibility for Hitler and yet another war. Responsibility for the loss of many thousands of British lives: countless numbers of our allies. They shared the guilt of Slave Labour and the horrendous evil of the Gas Chambers. Oh Yes, I was aware of all this. Only *too well* aware!

However, when fingering those pink-ribboned bundles of precious letters at Flaesheim I wondered if that young fraulein would ever again meet her lover.

I still wonder if he came back.

I *hope* so!

Bridge over the Ems

The wrecked bridge had carried the main railway line to the Ruhr. Priority of reconstruction was vital for restoring communications desperately needed to service the advance.

An overall survey for getting the line operational in the hands of an American, reconnoitring its length it was found this particular bridge over the Ems to be probably the biggest blown up by German Engineers and Pioneers in retreat. Two massive stone built piers, all that was left, loomed skywards between steep banks.

Specialising in railway reconstruction and having achieved some reputation it was little surprise the hundred or so Pioneers required would be drawn from our company, to work with a platoon of Sappers.

When the news of the assignment came through, nominated to take this detachment, very reluctantly the loan of the utility van and driver had been released to me for the remainder of the day for an immediate 'look see', primarily, with accommodation in mind, to locate the nearest Town Major, known to be at Essen.

Essen was in a shocking mess, with homeless locals overcrowding the less badly blitzed houses.

The Town Major shrugged.

'One hundred men? No chance!'

A town map on the wall, he pointed to a nearby village.

'Have a look at the school there. It might be big enough'.

On arrival, the school was in full use.

It was obviously suitable.

Explaining the purpose of the visit to a matronly teacher, No, it would not be necessary for the school to close down. Out working for most of the day we would prefer the children to follow usual routine, and yes, they would be perfectly safe.

In her eyes, utter amazement! Still expressing her gratitude, the District Nurse stormed in ready to give any support and vigorous verbal defence the situation called for. Invariably, wherever the Allies advanced, the District Nurse, true to the profession, had remained behind.

First glimpse of the kids suggested most of them had ricketts. In a rural area bordering on Recklinghausen this was puzzling.

'Surely' it was ventured 'with the abundance of farms around here, you locals, particularly the children, have been able to get a reasonable amount of the right food?'

'Nein, Nein!' came the combined reply.

Apparently, throughout the War years all food had been carted away.

Time important, it was necessary to re-visit the Essen Town Major, 'book' the school, and push on with the return journey back to Company quarters.

Again explaining a hundred men would move in on the morrow, that the school must carry on, in saying Goodbye, two fraus joyfully repeated 'Danke-schons!'

Then surprisingly, it was the District Nurse speaking.

'Will you please?'

'Ja?'

'Will you take my typewriter?'

'Warum?'

'German policeman here stealing everything'.

Pulling out a scruffy copy of Second Army Newsletter the top official-looking part bearing the blue and white heraldic shield was torn off, and a receipt scribbled. Jointly prompted by the fraus a German translation was added in capitals.

'Show him this. And tell him I'm coming to see him tomorrow! But hide the typewriter!'

More danke-schons!

With a wave to the women and the pitifully wan small children we were off, with the danke-schons echoing above the tilly's engine noise.

Those kids were to become the luckiest in Deutschland.

Pioneers adopted the lot!

NAAFI rations heaped on them!

Real chocolate. Real sweets!

For the school to operate, a routine quickly emerged. Breakfast over, all palliases piled high in one corner, leaving the main hall clear.

One typewriter was packed away in Stores, to be returned when we moved on.

The detachment was received with much curiosity and extraordinary courtesy by the villagers.

The innkeeper sought an interview. A Brewery nearby, could authority be issued for materials to enable production to re-start? On the understanding one hundred British needs would first be supplied, after suitable negotiations the beer arrived. Situated some few hundred yards from the school the Innkeeper had the unexpected satisfaction of seeing his bierzimmer repaired free of charge, transformed into the Unit's clubroom. There would also prove to be sufficient surplus beer for him to do up a back room and allow limited opening for civilians. Everybody was happy!

Technicalities and materials for the railway bridge reconstruction had been well pre-planned.

Whilst work proceeded on repairing the fabric of the piers, stores rapidly accumulated, including huge and heavy steel spanning girders.

Ready for the girders, only volunteers would act as spidermen. It would be a long drop to the water! What an awesome sight watching the first girder precariously hanging and being placed into position!

Temperature in the eighties, stripped to the waist Sappers and Pioneers worked unrecognisably together. A few bodies did hurtle down. Suspiciously by intent! Before long, during breaks, with everybody in the water, the more adventuresome were diving or jumping from the girders, luckily without casualty!

Work continued apace for perhaps a fortnight, when, picking his way down the slope, binoculars swinging, came the solitary figure of the U.S. red tab charged with getting the line operative.

'Hi there friends! How's it going? Touring the whole line. When can you be ready?' Informed within about forty-eight hours, he was off with a cheery wave, volubly expressing appreciation. It seemed pointless to enquire his name.

Finally completed, more by way of congratulation than celebration it would be necessary to fully inspect. This, a problem! No ordinary stretch of railroad, the 'sleepers' straddling the girders had been set much further apart than a short-legged Resident Pioneer officer could manage! Sitting on a main girder and shuffling across, daft as it was, seemed the only possible way. The very considerable daylight between sleepers didn't help. Attempted, conscious of the many upturned faces below, and all the laughing encouragement, vertigo-in-excelsis struck! Quite definitely I was not going to cross that bridge! Hands lost grip; forehead resting on steel, complete paralysis took over. In such plight all one could do was balance and hope for the best! When composure returned, a backwards shuffle, to much cheering, and terra firma! One's first experience of how crippling vertigo can be, as anyone so afflicted will testify!

All was now ready for the opening of the line.

A test engine arrived.

Horrified at the flat structure, the open gaps between sleepers, the German civilian driver and his mate positively refused to venture!

The alternative was to contact Railway Operating Group and obtain a pukka Sapper crew. Urgency demanded immediate but not so gentle persuasion.

Revolver in hand the instruction was brief and simple.

'Gehen Sie! Schnell! Schnell!'

That bridge would have to take many heavy train loads and I had every confidence in Sapper mathematics.

Sergeants were now shoving the protesting crew up on to the foot-plate, holding them there.

The instruction was repeated, and for the last time, or they would be shot.

White-faced, terrified, two Germans refused to move.

Clambering aboard, the revolver was pressed into the driver's back. He wasn't to know, unloaded! Murdering the German language, at least they fully understood, and were mightly glad to have the assurance:

'Ich will kommen mit Sie!'

Everybody understood that!

And a further distortion of the German language.

'Velleich wir alles tote suzammen! Jezst! Gehen! Schnell!'

I stayed aboard.

Fortunately it worked!

Very slowly the engine inched on to the heavy flat un-bridge like structure, and on reaching the opposite bank immediately braked to a halt, bringing relief to not two, but three occupants!

Eagerly and gratefully, driver and mate stretched trembling hands towards the proffered packet of English cigarettes!

That night the War Lords would have celebrated too!

And, who knows? Maybe a special cigar lit up!

Map-Reading Blunder

In strange open country, in passenger seat, map on lap, always is most fascinating.

'In about a mile there'll be a church'.

'Soon, over on our right, a lake of sorts'.

'Couple of miles, we go under a bridge'.

The realisation always so pleasing!

But as everybody knows, map-reading is dead easy! Simple as reading a book!

To cope with the rapid advance into Germany, Mobile Depots had been sent out. Rations, Army Post, Ordnance, Field Cashiers, and of course NAAFI. These could be anywhere. Literally. Only by travelling around and making enquiries could they be found.

Moving into a new location, whether in bivvies, tents, or the more preferred shelter of damaged buildings, always there was the drill of going through the initial list of priorities.

The Company's rations – its daily food – paramount. Mail and NAAFI supplies high on the list. Not far behind, a football pitch!

Any 'Town Major' could be helpful. Somebody might have reported having seen or heard of a particular mobile supply parked somewhere or heading in a given direction. It was always a case of search and find! Taking a chance! Having a hunch!

The spur to find constantly there!

To hare back with a bundle of special mail, see faces light up as names announced, this the greatest joy of all!

Travelling perhaps a hundred-mile round journey along lonely, often devastated, roads and fastening on to mail or NAAFI rations brought delight and rewards which cannot possibly be expressed in words. We were a happy Company. Miserable days and nights encouraged the urge for these forays, many completely unsuccessful!

It didn't need a 'trick-cyclist' to explain!

Instinctively, all could recognise genuine effort and any 'bull' smelt a mile away! Those responsible who were not exactly dedicated to the cause were sniffed out with unerring accuracy!

The average Second-in-Command knew what was expected of him. Supposedly off-duty, should he catch up on much needed sleep or should he respond to the temptation, the thrill, the possible satisfaction, of just one more 'recce'? Westwards yesterday, maybe northwards today?

On such outings rank and official relationships more often than not went by the board. Explorers shared the same challenge. Two mates, one mission.

Unhesitatingly into the unknown the tilly van driver steered to the word of the map-reader; both equally over the moon should good fortune produce two lots of mail and double-contrived NAAFI rations on the same trip!

It was a fine warm afternoon. Good to be out in open country!

The road ahead was long, straight and devoid of any special landmark.

An absence of 'Woodlands to the right' suggested the map might be an old one. Maybe trees had been felled wholesale in some war effort?

'Distinct fork – take the left' proved a very definite T-junction. Well, possibly there could have been some new road construction?

'Hill on right, with large schloss'.

No hill. No schloss!

'Keep going: could be a bit further on!'

The road fizzled out, becoming an unsurfaced lane.

'Funny! This is supposed to be a main road!'

The lane viraged around aimlessly for a couple of miles.

'I think we're lost' admitted the mapreader.

'I'm damn sure!' grimaced the driver.

Impossible to retrace steps: we'd come too far for that. Yes, agreed. No option but to push on. Perhaps we'd meet someone to quiz. Perhaps stumble upon some recognisable feature and get re-orientated!

The lane narrowed to a dusty foot-track, hardly wide enough for any vehicle. At a bend it rose to an overgrown escarpment. Barging through this, suddenly below was a stream, across which a makeshift footbridge of railway sleepers.

'Must lead somewhere!' breathed the driver.

'Think you can get acr . . .?'

Question unfinished, the van shot down the bank, on to the sleepers and up the other side! A further abrupt turn and the track followed the stream. At a rise in the ground, through trees and scrub, a distinct village was glimpsed. Good! We'd soon know which, and find it on the map!

The track circumvented a large field. Deeply rutted. Clearly, only farm tractors had ventured this way.

A tall wild hedge obscured the view, but on rising ground, at a gate, we stopped to size up how best to get into the village.

Quite a number of men were leisurely strolling around. Military vehicles were dotted here and there. And tanks. The slant of the afternoon sun didn't help but battle-dressed figures less than two hundred yards away suddenly seemed so much nearer. They were in German grey-green!

Heedless of what may have been in the long grass the driver flung the van round in a complete circle and careered back along the track, chancing a broken axle! Back to cover. Back to the sleeper bridge, which at reverse viewing seemed to have shrunk even narrower. Speeding across, clearance must have been fractional; the driving immaculate.

Not a word was spoken.

Accelerating hard, the outgoing route was re-traced. Not a vehicle in sight. Not even a cyclist. Not a soul! This no longer strange!

Twenty minutes passed before the silence was broken.

'Think we've left 'em behind?' grinned the driver.

'Yup!' breathed a relieved occupant of the passenger seat.

Ahead were the comforting colours of British and Canadian Unit signboards.

Time for a laugh, and the exchange of the what-might-have-been!

'And how did you manage to become a POW?' quizzed the officer.

'Oh! No heroics! Couple of us crazily drove over and gave ourselves up!' answered the driver.

Nothing was brought back from any Mobile Unit that day. But there *would* be a tomorrow!

The low evening sun dazzled on the windscreen.

'No Mans Land' had been really beautiful.

The driver summed up the day's foray beautifully too!

'Blimey!' he chortled 'we can recognise Jerries but we can't bloody well map read!'

Slave Labour

Road transport could not possibly cope with getting supplies and ammunition up to the forward troops. It was imperative to get the railway lines functioning. Engineers and Pioneers were pushed up in numbers.

Coesfeld, once a quiet pleasant German town was ruined, but bristling, and absorbing an astonishing variety of Units such as RASC, REME and the like.

On the end walls of wrecked terraced houses could be seen the remains of the huge white painted customary Nazi exhortation to fight for its defence to the last man. 'Jedes Mann, Jedes Haus, Alles fur Den Fürher!'

At this stop, large drying sheds of a brickworks would afford protection for the Company's tentage making erection of the outer 'flies' unnecessary.

A single brick garage at the Works entrance quite naturally became the Orderly Office. This faced the brickworks owner's splendid private house now harbouring a considerable number of evacuees from the nearby town.

Remarkably the brickworks had remained undamaged.

Siting of canvas agreed, Sergeants were busily directing proceedings. Time for a tour!

First, to the big house.

'Shtinkintrauser', as he became known, invited the small inspection party in for drinks. This waived aside, he would accompany us immediately, starting at his double garage. It was locked. Herr 'S' was hastened to fetch the key, and all others.

Hesitatingly, the garage doors were opened.

Inside was a draped car. Yes, he did hold a military permit, and produced a piece of paper signed by an American, explaining that as rebuilding some time in the future would be vital it had been agreed the car was necessary for him to keep an eye on three other brickworks he owned in the area. Logical perhaps, but why so much dust on the cover? The answer was simple. Petrol rationing to civilians had stopped some time ago, though the Americans did let him have a little.

Unwilling removal of the shroud revealed a shiny black Mercedes-Benz. Expressing doubts about the petrol we hurried to survey the whole of the Works and various outbuildings.

The tour was drawing to an end.

Some two hundred yards away across waste land, well clear of the brickworks stood a tall substantial brick building.

'Yours?'

'Ja mein herrn'.

Walking towards this, increasingly, there was an indefinably peculiar smell. Nasty and pungent.

With the unlocking of an end door a sickening musty odour oozed out.

At the sight inside, stomachs overturned.

A completely unimaginable jungle of filth!

The walls windowless, what had been tiers of timber-compressed-together bunk beds reaching to the eaves were now hanging precariously, some completely smashed, obviously in anger, and for use as weapons. Broken battens lay scattered about in hopeless confusion amongst discarded dirty and ragged old clothing, blankets, footwear and other unwanted personal cast-offs.

And excreta everywhere!

Which told everything. Slave labour had been locked in, God knows how long, before liberation!

At the far end a solid single door, having a small glass inspection point, stood shut. Without doubt the guardroom.

Why, it was demanded of Schtinkintrauser, had the place been allowed to become so grossly fouled? And where were the toilets?

He led us fifty yards away and pointed to one small open hole in the ground. At least two hundred miserable wretches must have been squeezed into that prison.

'Is this the only latrine?'

'Ja'.

'What about washing?'

A lone standpipe with tap was pointed out.

'Only cold water?'

'Ja mein herrn'.

'For more than two hundred people?'

'Ja'.

Twenty-four hours! That's what he was given to get the whole building completely clear of the nauseating indescribable mess. All to be burnt!

No! No! he protested: he couldn't do any manual work. Hadn't got any men. We'd only been in there one minute and had to leave! No, No, he couldn't possibly . . .

'Twenty-four hours! Or we lock you in there for a week, then we shoot you. Tote! Kaput!'

Terrified, he scuttled off.

Returning to the bustling activity within the drying sheds, the Major was duly briefed.

'Yes' he murmured 'saw him chase off in a small yellow car'.

'Yellow car Major? Shtinkintrauser?'

'Certain!'

Two hours later, a creeping black pall of acrid smoke signalled some activity at the DP building. It transpired some civilians had been rounded up and ferried in via a back approach road.

The Sarntmajor volunteered to go over and make sure Herr 'S' was himself inside, taking a full part in the dirty work. The S.M. would also bring him back for interview at the house garage.

No time was wasted.

'American Permit. Show it!'

Taken from him, the registration number was loudly read out.

'NOT for THIS car?'

'Nein, mein herrn'.

'For the small French car – the yellow one?'

'Ja mein herrn'.

'You're a filthy liar too, Ja?'

'Ja mein herrn'.

'Right! We'll deal with you later. Now get back to work!'

He was propelled in the right direction.

The Mercedes-Benz was commandeered.

Gleefully, the Company's small MT staff stayed up the whole of that night experimenting in an attempt to turn the engine over. No wonder! The Merc, it was discovered, had been laid up since before September 1939! Petrol rationing had been even more strict than in Britain!

Montgomery, it so happened, had just forbidden any further requisitioning of vehicles of any kind. German civil life would somehow have to recover and some transport essential.

To regularise matters the Company Clerk eagerly helped. Shoving paper into his typewriter a certificate emerged for sticking on the Merc's windscreen, reading:

'I have today (...date) freely and willingly gifted this car, Registration No... to my British friend (...rank and name) ... (signed).'

Repeated to the best ability in German, this was sent over to the house for required attention.

Dishevelled and distressed, Herr 'S' showed himself at the door of Company Office, pleading for mercy, over-anxious to return the document duly signed, and to report all contents of the DP building had been removed and burnt.

'Now you wash all floor and walls' snapped the 2 i/c.

'And get some disinfectant!' added the Major.

The yellow Citroen again shot off to collect the civilians. Where and how he got the petrol another story.

The horrendous building was eventually locked and put out of bounds. Nobody who glimpsed its ghastly contents could ever forget. Although worse was to be seen, this first evidence of Slave Labour was the most shocking.

With dedication and mechanical wizardry, though using more oil than petrol the Mercedes was made roadworthy. Colourfully bedecked with Second Army, 21st Army Group and 30 Corps flashes it looked magnificent! Important too! Mistaken for some very very high ranking individual, approaching any crossroads all other traffic invariably halted! The Merc always waived through to the flourish of a Redcap salute, with front occupant embarrassingly hiding below dashboard level!

But a really genuine VIP did call in at the brickworks one evening. Leisurely standing at the flap of the Major's tent, apologising and introducing himself. Unaccompanied, a most senior American red tab. Greetings over, he squatted down to explain his visit.

'Gentlemen, together we must restore some kind of order. These Russian DP's going berserk! Mayhem! After all, folk round here just like those way back home . . . salt of the earth! Will you please co-operate and always have an armed posse ready?'

Of plundering DP's on the rampage we well knew! On our first day's arrival a local farming family had deposited the dead body of their father, as proof, on the floor of Company office. Messengers from farms and hamlets had continually begged protection.

Gangs of a hundred, two hundred, marauders were terrifying, raping, killing, stealing, burning and generally hell-bent on reaping revenge. When the reports came in we did what we could, but always it was too late: they'd moved on for further pillage.

Yes, we agreed with the American, our efforts would be stepped up though transport posed a serious problem. He could not believe a Pioneer Company's MT availability was so limited – expressed great surprise as to how we managed at all – but No! Couldn't see how he could help with any vehicles!

Search and find armed parties were duly sent out using whatever transport available – more often than not the water-cart! Stuck and bogged down on one occasion in a farm lane, in a somewhat foolish rush of blood half the contents were run off to lighten the load. A complete disaster!

A helpful farmer rustled up all available horses from neighbouring farms. Adding two by two they were hitched up. It took eight magnificent steeds to eventually yank the water cart from the sea of mud, much to the relief of one red-faced officer and the considerable amusement of half a dozen riflemen.

Some gangs were cornered, leaders seized, the mob split into smaller parties and escorted off in different directions. All we could do. These ringleaders were dumped on to the American outfit in the next village. One had achieved considerable notoriety. Dubbed 'Stalinski' we had nailed him and half-expected some kind of appreciation from the high ranking visitor. To our dismay Stalinski was spotted walking alone along the main road. This called for some explanation. Visiting the American camp, the Sergeant in charge of the prison unconcernedly drawled the explanation.

'Yeah – we frisked him. Took loads of watches and loot, but Jees, the place is full up! Pushed him off!'

We left the Yank infantry to get on with it, and concentrated on our main task of rail construction!

Very soon another move was notified; which was timely! The red dust of the brick drying sheds harboured the breeding ground of strange-looking fleas. The Company unofficial barber was working overtime to compete – delicately!

The Merc? It was left where found. Some NCOs wanted to set it alight or chuck a grenade in its engine. It was however very thoroughly immobilised.

Travels took us close up to the advancing infantry. We were to come across more and more of the just-abandoned DP hovels, some small, some large.

We'd seen and heard more than enough of Displaced Persons, Slave Labour and Jewish pogroms!

At the gates of Belsen Concentration Camp the large makeshift sign 'Please! Only Enter If On Business!' seemed so unnecessary. It was easy to comply.

Those atrocities were to stun the world. At the time, *we* were beyond being shocked!

LETTER

BY THE

COMMANDER-IN-CHIEF

ON

NON-FRATERNISATION

TO ALL OFFICERS AND MEN OF 21 ARMY GROUP

1. Twenty-seven years ago the Allies occupied Germany: but Germany has been at war ever since. Our Army took no revenge in 1918; it was more than considerate, and before a few weeks had passed many soldiers were adopted into German households. The enemy worked hard at being amiable. They believed that the occupation was due to treachery, and that their army had never been beaten. They remained unrepentant and attached to their worship of brute force.

2. The fight was continued by the German General Staff, who concealed war criminals and equipments, built up armaments, and trained a new striking force. To evade the Armistice terms they had to find sympathisers, and "organising sympathy" became a German industry. So accommodating were the occupying forces that the Germans came to believe we would never fight them again in any cause. From that moment to this their continued aggression has brought misery or death to millions, always under the familiar smoke screen of appeals for fair play and friendship, followed by the barrage of stark, brutal threats.

This time the Nazis have added to the experience of the last occupation; they have learned from the resistance movements of France, Belgium, Holland, and Norway. These are the type of instructions they are likely to give to their underground workers:

> "Give the impression of submitting. Say you never liked the Nazis; they were the people responsible for the war. Argue that Germany has never had a fair chance. Get the soldiers arguing; they are not trained for it, and you are.

> "Use old folks, girls, and children, and 'play up' every case of devastation or poverty. Ask the troops to your homes; sabotage or steal equipment, petrol or rations. Get troops to sell these things, if you can. Spread stories about Americans and Russians in the British zone, and about the British to other Allies."

3. Because of these facts, I want every soldier to be clear about "non-fraternisation". Peace does not exist merely because of a surrender. The Nazi influence penetrates everywhere, even into children's schools and churches. Our occupation of Germany is an act of war of which the first object is to destroy the Nazi system. There are Allied organisations whose work it is to single out, separate and destroy the dangerous elements in German life. It is too soon for you to distinguish between "good" and "bad" Germans: you have a positive part to play in winning the peace by a definite code of behaviour. In streets, houses, cafes, cinemas, etc., you must keep clear of Germans, man, woman and child, unless you meet them in the course of duty. You must not walk out with them, or shake hands, or visit their homes, or make them gifts, or take gifts from them. You must not play games with them or share any social event with them. In short, you must not fraternise with Germans at all.

4. To refrain from fraternisation is not easy. It requires self-discipline. But in Germany you will have to remember that laughing and eating and dancing with Germans would be bitterly resented by your own families, by millions of people who have suffered under the Gestapo and under the Luftwaffe's bombs, and by every Ally that Britain possesses. You will have to remember that these are the same Germans who, a short while ago, were drunk with victory, who were boasting what they as the Master Race would do to you as their slaves, who were applauding the utter disregard by their leaders of any form of decency or of honourable dealings: the same Germans whose brothers, sons and fathers were carrying out a system of mass murder and torture of defenceless civilians. You will have to remember that these same Germans are planning to make fools of you again and to escape the loathing which their actions deserve.

5. Our consciences are clear; "non-fraternisation" to us implies no revenge; we have no theory of master races. But a guilty nation must not only be convicted: it must realise its guilt. Only then can the first steps be taken to re-educate it, and bring it back into the society of decent humanity.

6. German discipline, though not our sort, is thorough. The people will judge you with no amateur eyes: and any slackness will be the cue for the resistance movements to intensify their efforts.

7. Be just; be firm; be correct; give orders, and don't argue. Last time we won the war and let the peace slip out of our hands. This time we must not ease off—we must win both the war and the peace.

B. L. Montgomery

Field-Marshal,
C-in-C 21 Army Group.

March, 1945.

PSS 1810 3.45

'Frat' Ban

On reaching Germany, over a space of time, to all in his Command, Montgomery issued personal card messages on how the Germans must be treated.

The most welcome, the last, heralded the end of Non-Fraternisation.

It may be of interest to place these three messages on record here.

The wider issues of the 'Frat' Ban and its lifting are voluminous. Suffice it to say that the War over, momentum lost, eyes turned to sport and leisure pursuits, a personal involvement with which at Company level led the writer progressively on to Group, then District responsibility and finally to the privilege of invitation to join Second Army HQ Central Sports Committee which met centrally somewhere. Was it Celle?

Obligations meant considerable travelling. If a motorbike couldn't be scrounged, hitch-hiking was the norm.

This channelling of energies put sport very much into the urgent bracket, and from the outset Committee members were kept fully stretched – particularly locating gear and equipment. Urgent orders went off to the U.K.

The message was simple.

Esprit-de-Corps, to be maintained, must be carried to the playing fields.

During those immediate post-War weeks perhaps the most ambitious single enterprise was an open-to-all gathering on Mini-Olympic lines, giving opportunity for the colours of every possible Regiment and Corps to be in evidence. A whole series of events was programmed and enthusiasm whipped up.

On the day, inter-Regimental, inter-Corps and even inter-Company pride at stake, quite naturally red and green Pioneer flashes were everywhere to be seen.

Most vividly remembered, the mile.

No real Olympics could possibly field the huge number of starters. The great roar as 'our' man was urged on! A roar which dissolved into stunned silence as hitting the tape in victory he dropped dead! We reckoned he really had died in action. Never before had he even run a mile! He just 'had a go'!

Well recalled too, another memorable 'first'. Germans in Wolfsburg invited to play soccer against one Pioneer Company on the

Volkswagen Motor Works' Sports Ground. An event which typically demonstrated that trait of German thoroughness.

Changed into soccer gear, we drove over to the venue with a somewhat weakened eleven, one or two, though obviously not fit, press-ganged into playing in this unique history-making encounter. After all, it was only a bit of fun and likely to be something of an exhibition game!

Civilians were on the streets in vast numbers. We wondered why.

Nearing the ground, amazingly, the whole population, men, women, children, swarmed along in the same direction! All going to the game! After years and years of unbroken gloom and hardship, nobody, just nobody, was going to miss out on this very first public entertainment! A sense of occasion was in the air! On arrival at the Sports Ground, thousands, half a dozen deep had already surrounded the pitch!

Later, it was learned the match had been very much publicized as no ordinary kick-about, but elevated to the status of Wolfsburg City versus THE British Army!!

A sporting contest saw victory for the locals. Our lads were completely shaken by the opposition's unbelievably high skills.

Local? For this first, very special opportunity, established German League footballers had been traced and imported in from hundreds of miles around, some taking several days to make the trip!

Civilian spirits took a mighty leap!

Montgomery could be sure his timing was right!

Thereafter, in Wolfsburg, occupying military forces could do no wrong. Civilian liaison, civil obedience, became 'dead easy'.

That first soccer match following the lifting of the 'Frat' Ban proved a marvellous master-stroke!

Does Sport help surmount international barriers?

At Wolfsburg, in 1945, there was no possible doubt whatever!

LETTER No. 2

BY THE

COMMANDER-IN-CHIEF

ON

NON-FRATERNISATION

TO ALL MEMBERS OF 21 ARMY GROUP

1. I have been considering the present orders about non-fraternisation.

We cannot let-up on this policy.

2. But these orders need no longer apply to small children.

3. Members of the British Forces in Germany will be allowed to speak to, and play with, little children. This will come into effect at once. In all other respects the orders issued by me in the card dated March 1945 will remain in force.

B. L. Montgomery

Field Marshal,
C-in-C, 21 Army Group.

12 June 1945.

LETTER No. 3

BY THE

COMMANDER-IN-CHIEF

ON

NON-FRATERNISATION

TO ALL MEMBERS OF THE BRITISH FORCES IN GERMANY

Great progress has been made in the de-Nazification of the British Zone and in removing Nazis from all responsibility in German life. Further, the Germans have shown themselves willing to obey my orders and to co-operate in the reconstruction of their country on non-Nazi lines.

I have already modified my orders about non-fraternisation and allowed you to speak and play with little children. I now consider it desirable and timely to permit a further modification of these rules. You may now engage in conversation with adult Germans in the streets and in public places.

You will not for the present enter the homes and houses of the Germans nor permit them to enter any of the premises you are using except for duty or work.

I know the non-fraternisation policy has been a strain upon many of you who have to live and work in close contact with Germans, and I appreciate the loyal way in which you have honoured it.

B. L. Montgomery

Field Marshal,
Commander-in-Chief,
British Zone.

14 July 45.

The Main Predator

Death was rarely talked about.

Jokingly, yes!

'If your number's on it, that's it!'

The ever-present possibility would never influence or interrupt what became accepted as normal daily activity. Like animals hunting in packs almost everyone became totally unafraid of, and could ignore, the main predator.

Infantry, the spearhead, walked closer. Always holding deep admiration for those in front it was not ours to advance and kill or be killed.

But of course death was far from being unfamiliar to Support troops.

Many had seen active service with Infantry. Death was not unfamiliar to them. Nor to the recently enlisted who had been on the end of Goering's blitzing of home cities and towns.

A number of our own mob had witnessed whole squads of comrades blown to bits whilst going about the mundane job of railway construction: shocked to see nearby billets eliminated, taking almost the whole personnel of a sister-Company: some had seen wholesale carnage at the direct hit of an Antwerp cinema: others had been attached to Military Cemeteries.

Death was familiar. The dead had been carried away. Given all that, others would have had minds concentrated when jostling lorry-bound through the Nijmegen area faced with the litter of gliders and aircraft standing as memorials pointing skywards from whence those Airborne boys had come; and further up plunged dangerously off the road to pass crippled German tanks, blond heads slumped from cockpits – left untouched in case booby trapped.

Oh yes! Your average support troops were well familiar with death.

Typically so, one Sergeant Thornton.

Streams of tanks and other military traffic moving non-stop towards the Rhine, he dodged across the flow and clambered over rubble piled house-high, bulldozed aside to make passage possible through Goch. There had been a fierce and bloody battle here.

Beneath his feet, Sergeant T caught a whisper of what might have been the squeal of a rat. It did however have an eeriness which puzzled and alerted him. Scrambling back he listened intently. Very faintly he heard the same peculiar squeak. Something instinctive urged him into action.

All traffic halted, silence called for, it was as though the war had stopped. Reminiscent of those previous Novembers when on the 11th at the eleventh hour everything ground to a halt.

But this silence was not for the dead.

Drivers, curious, tiptoed to join him.

Yes! the Sergeant was sure. It was a human cry!

Word spread quickly. Comrades arrived to find Sergeant T and others tearing away by hand large slabs of brickwork and all the flotsam and jetsam of household wreckage. Many hands were soon helping, each slab carefully removed and props fashioned to hold up the debris.

Stench overpowering, speed was essential.

In the rubbish and filth the blackened upright body of a woman was located in what could have been the remants of a pantry. At her feet a small bundle, a baby, alive, crying.

High on top of the rubble civilians had gathered to watch. Some were despatched to find the District Nurse. From these onlookers it was gleaned an incredible fifteen days had gone by since the last shelling and bombing!

Gently extricated to the comforting sound of foreign voices an almost unrecognisable bundle passed along a line of Pioneers to the arms of one bystander sobbingly explaining she was a relative.

A small much begrimed party hi-jacked a lorry and hastened to the nearest British M.O.

Sergeant Thornton directed the whole humanitarian operation. He it was who started it. His personal responsibility, he saw things through to the end. Arrangements made to give the mother a decent burial, he took himself off to check on how that dirty little bundle had been cleaned up.

It was a couple of days before we heard anything at all about this and could piece things together.

Sergeant T was a tough character. He was also modestly uncommunicative. Tackled about the babe, in a mixture of emotion and elation he did manage a few words.

'Just been up there again. She's going to *LIVE!!* District Nurse told me!' he said.

Specialists Wanted!

Second Echelon HQ comfortably based way back at one of the Channel ports, and later Brussels, was regarded as our Civil Service, pouring out admin directions which would eventually reach forward Units constantly on the move. The amount of paper received at Company level via local Group HQ really was astonishing. Amongst this lot were regular requests for 'Specialists'.

Despite its long and proud history the stark fact was the British Army seemed wholly unprepared for eventualities! Speedy movement was something quite unfamiliar, bringing demands undreamed of, and extremely serious gaps.

The cream of specialized Units were already up front. Any withdrawal from these outfits just not on! In the wake, problems were accumulating needing particular skills: men of action, decision takers, who were just not available. Resort was made to circularising all Units, wherever they might be, on a blanket basis, with exhortations to root out and release individuals whose earlier civil experience could be applied to specific urgent needs.

Truth was, the Allies were becoming Occupying Powers without the means of management! Whole cities and towns were in ruins and bereft of normally indigenous key figures. Sewage, Gas, Electricity, road and rail communications, hospitals, all these and other essential needs somehow must be restored and maintained, but where find men to grapple with these problems?

Penetrating into Germany itself, OC's, naturally, were reluctant to respond by nominating, and volunteering to lose, experienced colleagues and staff. Many appeals were deliberately 'mislaid'.

The Ruhr Coalfields had been overrun. Fuel vital, somehow things had to be started up again . . . production and distribution tackled. The official appeal for those with suitable experience was so important all the bumph was emphasised in capital letters and underlined, spotting which, a whiff of mercurial promotion caught in the nostrils! Coal technology, mines, shipping and distribution had been my life!

In anticipation of the end of hostilities the Release Group Demobilisation scheme had been made known, from which it was apparent I would be stuck in the Army for some time ahead, and when Germany *did* surrender goodness knows what the future might bring! Perhaps it might be wise to slot into the Ruhr Coalfields set-up? Getting in on the ground floor might well ease the financial lot of my family too! Besides which, many new Majors with no field experience whatever were being brought up – the new Company's OC one of them.

Yes! It would be most timely!

Slapping in an application hopefully expecting it would not be sabotaged at source, with procrastination allowed for, a couple of weeks would almost certainly see some development.

Within days, and probably before Second Echelon could have received my offer, amongst circulars received there came a 'splash' from Monty himself. From all supporting Units in Germany forty officers to be nominated for immediate transfer to Infantry.

'Rocky', a colleague, professional footballer and extremely fit, we agreed would almost certainly be one to go. Our new friendship would be short-lived. He found some consolation in the assurance that postings would be to the Regiment of choice providing this already in Germany, but couldn't think why. He sought some advice.

'Go for the Gordons. You'll look fine in a kilt!'

'Not a bad idea' he said 'I'll keep it in mind!'

The Group Instruction of Posting arrived which confirmed Rocky had indeed been named.

But surprise! surprise! It was in duplicate.

The second copy carried my own name!

A Group Colonel undoubtedly had remembered a little sorté in which I had been involved and felt I ought to be doing the same thing on a regular basis. How daft! Should I enlighten him? What would Schweik do?

But of course! Obey the last order!

The two of us travelled many miles back together to Termonde, where it was spelled out, quite definitely, 'as from now' each man could consider himself on the books of whatever the personally-chosen Regiment.

'I'm wi' you, in the Gordon Highlanders!' chanted Rocky, affecting a Scots lilt.

We kipped down in a barn to be ready for the supposed formality of an early morning interview which in effect was a one-man War Office Selection Board; the one man being Col. Alexander, elder brother of the General.

He greeted me brusquely.

'Take those bloody glasses off!'

The specs were removed.

'Bluff, and unworthy!' he added.

'Sir, to try and kid you wouldn't occur to me'.

He was not a man to waste time.

Leaning forwards, face to face, his attitude changed to the conversational.

'How long you been wearing 'em?'

'Since a child Sir'.

'What's wrong with that right eye?'

'Regrettably, almost blind'.

'Why the hell are you graded A1?'

'Normal on commissioning Sir'.

'You were in the ranks?'

'Yes sir'.

'What grade were you then?'

'B4'.

'Who sent you here?'

'Group Colonel sir'.

'Knows you wear those things!'

'He does'.

'Christ! A bit of dust in one eye and men's lives would be at risk – you must know that!'

'I do understand that sir'.

'Gordon Highlanders indeed! Thanks for coming, but bugger off!'

The interview over, I was at the door.

'And tell that Colonel he's a bloody fool' were the last words from Col. Alexander.

With mixed feelings, not wishing for idle chat with the others, and without saying goodbye to Rocky, I was outside hitching a lift. Many hitches and many hours later within a short walk of the Company I had no wish to rejoin.

A staff car was approaching; the Group Colonel seated in front. Impossible to pretend I hadn't noticed him. The required compliment was blatantly unacknowledged. To say the least I was unexpected!

Plodding on, it was not difficult to imagine his confusion! Without glancing behind I knew the car had stopped and turned round. It drew up beside me.

'You're supposed to be at . . . at . . .' he challenged.

'Been there Sir!'

'But . . . but . . . why are you back?' he spluttered.

'RTU'd Sir'.

'RTU'd? On whose authority?' he demanded.

'Colonel Alexander, sir, brother of the General'.

'Alexander . . . Alexander did you say?'

'Yes indeed Sir. And O Yes! He did casually ask me to pass on a personal word to you Sir!'

Reacting to being linked with the famous, so consumed with his own importance, he assumed an air of modesty.

'Really? We have met of course. What did he say?'

The moment of truth had arrived! This must be carefully prolonged, and savoured!

With Schweik within urging mischievously on, Colonel Alexander's condemnation came out. Very deliberately and very slowly.

'Colonel-Alexander-asked-me-to-tell-you-Sir-you-are-a-bloody-fool!'

Choking a laugh the driver dropped his face to the wheel. Livid, the Colonel threw out an arm knocking both their caps askew. Had he been able to reach with the other arm my cap would have gone too!

Words would not come.

His face contorted. Purpled.

Froth oozed from snarling lips; he was dribbling down the chin; eyes bulging in disbelief – deliberating whether first to reach for a handkerchief or adjust his cap. Both accomplished, with a deep intake of breath, the order came in high pitched, almost crying falsetto.

'Drive on!'

With an approving wink to me the driver obeyed.

Of course, to put it mildly, I would be a marked man!

Admittedly, in complying with the most basic military requirement – always to obey the last order – this had offended unwritten etiquette demanding personal matters between officers never to be within a ranker's hearing.

Whatever the confliction, in the special circumstances I was sure I'd got priorities right, and that good soldier Schweik would have agreed! *He* got away with confounding a whole Polish Army!

Bare and very exposed, an early posting was awaited!

Pity about those Coal Commission people having let me slip through their fingers though!

The Old Story

Some good souls might object and should skip this. It concerns sex and promiscuity.

Somebody knows the facts, but it was widely believed that bromide, or some similar anti-aphrodisiac, was laced into the tea issue. With what effect open to question.

'Frat' ban lifted, local frauleins had been invited to attend the very first organised public dance.

The ball over, threading one's way across Luneberg Heath, avoiding prostrate bodies, a firm resolution was born.

Some attempt must be made to contact Horrocks – he who gave his name to the chemical pack, contents of which unfailingly went into those water tanks, mobile. A demand would be put in for a supply of prophylactics.

Searching for the hospital at which it was rumoured he had his headquarters, the first enemy troops to surrender approached. They were waved on: the immediate mission far more important!

Horrocks unavailable, a bemused RAMC Colonel reluctantly parted with the total known stock of the Second Army. Two hundred to be exact!

Discussing how distribution of such a miserable haul would not be interpreted as giving official encouragement, and to allow some measure of privacy, it was agreed to put up a small roughly constructed 'Proph. Shed' in the vicinity of the Company's field privvies.

Inside, suitable warning notices pinned up, the small box of preventatives which had taken so much time and trouble to obtain, were placed on a small table. A final lecture, and the place was opened. From a suitable distance the demand discreetly monitored.

Within minutes somebody had pinched the lot!

Yes, of course it had been a mistake.

Ah well, an effort had been made.

Sad to reflect, isn't it, that of all those who went through the Staff Training College at Camberley nobody had the vision to anticipate these circumstances?

All the prodigious and expensive work of The Army School of Hygiene had gone down the drain!

Once again, and 'orribly so, the British Army had been caught with its pants down!

Blowing in the Wind

The wind whistled its way carrying that now familiar all-pervading peculiar German stench through the town's rubble and dust.

Litter was flying about.

As were aircraft of the Allied Expeditionary Force.

Infantry ahead was in combat with massed fanatical, German troops defending the Rhine.

A small piece of coloured paper blew into my face. A printed leaflet. A glance showed it to be signed by Eisenhower.

Folded, it was stuffed into a battledress pocket.

I still have it.

A Surrender Pass. On the reverse side a resumé in German of the Geneva and Hague Convention rules.

Many British infantry and support troops would have witnessed those Safe Conduct Passes floating down by the thousand into beleaguered enemy lines.

Blowing in the wind that day, a scrap of paper which unmistakeably foretold the end was in sight!

Passierschein

(GÜLTIG FÜR EINEN ODER MEHRERE ÜBERBRINGER)

Der deutsche Soldat, der diesen Passierschein vorzeigt, benutzt ihn als Zeichen seines ehrlichen Willens, sich zu ergeben. Er ist zu entwaffnen. Er muß gut behandelt werden. Er hat Anspruch auf Verpflegung und, wenn nötig, ärztliche Behandlung. Er wird so bald wie möglich aus der Gefahrenzone entfernt.

DWIGHT D. EISENHOWER
Oberbefehlshaber
der Alliierten Streitkräfte

Englische Übersetzung nachstehend. Sie dient als Anweisung an die alliierten Vorposten.

SAFE CONDUCT

(VALID FOR ONE OR SEVERAL BEARERS)

The German soldier who carries this safe conduct is using it as a sign of his genuine wish to give himself up. He is to be disarmed, to be well looked after, to receive food and medical attention as required, and to be removed from the danger zone as soon as possible.

DWIGHT D. EISENHOWER
Supreme Commander,
Allied Expeditionary Force

Only One Nazi

Astonishingly, a couple of German soldiers, arms raised in surrender, were approaching. They were told to keep walking. Our vehicle was soon heading past groups of three or four, equally ignored. The groups grew into a steady trickle, the trickle into a vast shuffling, miserable procession crowding the road, including a small pony and trap on which privileged officers incongruously perched. As far as the eye could see we were surrounded by a whole Division, demoralised, silent, flooding along in complete dejection. All so totally unexpected!

We knew the end was in sight, but not *so* soon!

The concentration of effort in reconstruction of railway lines, all that laborious mundane lifting and packing of maintenance, now brought the extra dividend of dispersal of this wretched multitude.

The station platform already crowded for the first movement, ever obedient to orders, urged to move further along, this lot of the Wermacht pressed even more closely together. How difficult to realise this ragbag of dishevelled tramps, now POW, was once the mighty Germany Army which had blitzed, pillaged, terrorised and conquered!

It was almost unnecessary to call for attention.

When the train came in they would board only when instructed. This followed by an unpremeditated comment to a colleague.

'Look! Not a Nazi amongst the lot!'

Surprisingly, one voice was raised in reply.

'Ich bin ein Nazi!'

It was a hatless, typically Teuton, blond haired good looking youngster.

Beckoning him to come forward, he had one almighty struggle to get through his fellows to reach us.

More loudly, it was impossible to resist both a scathing yet admiring announcement.

'Here is an honest Nazi! The ONLY one!'

Spontaneously producing from a battledress tunic pocket whatever was left of a twenty packet of cigarettes this was handed to our solitary Nazi; likewise a box of matches.

His face broke into an appreciative, almost apologising, smile. He was utterly perplexed.

'O danke schon, Danke schon!' came repeatedly.

'Nicht forgessen?' was about all I could manage.

'Nicht forgessen, mein herr, nicht forgessen' saying which our honest Nazi was off in triumph.

Trivial incident – but perhaps he *did* remember!

The Burgermeister

With 21 Army Group in the BLA wherever a Pioneer Company moved, depending on the location, attachment to a particular Corps would be determined, though in our case for the most part the flash worn would be that of 30 Corps – black boar rampant on white background.

Sometimes a posting would mean a quick change, maybe to 1st Corps – the strikingly white spearhead on red.

Reaching Germany things became increasingly unclear as to which we officially belonged. Not that it mattered much. A glance at troops around and we simply made a choice, though on occasion, quite ridiculously , flashes of both 1st and 30 Corps stayed 'up'.

Always however the one insignia which remained a fixture was the familiar Second Army white shield armorial with blue cross of Lorraine carrying gold inverted sword.

Lines of Communication became more and more obscure and involved. An administrative mix up in which some Companies were 'lost', each obliged to survive solo, making its own decisions.

When moving up there was always a tacit, though flexible, routine.

Answerable to RE Railway Constructions, the first of the pre-requisites a courtesy call on the RE specialists to check expectations and area of likely operations. This would invariably be undertaken by a small advance party, pioneers in the true sense of the word, who would also find and establish living quarters.

If, as frequently, in a rural area where no Town major would be ensconced, it was off to see the nearest Burgermeister, should there be one.

Contact with the Burgermeister assumed special importance. Usually an elder of the community he often stayed on to meet and liaise with incoming Allied support troops. Whatever he might have evilly conspired earlier to make our presence miserable, generally speaking he would assist as much as he could.

Immediate past weeks would have been painfully difficult for him: his domain in chaos bringing problems of magnitude far beyond him. He could now resist the clamouring pleas of civilians by insisting he was helpless having abdicated responsibility to occupying British troops, though managing to retain authority of position in the eyes of locals by acting as spokesman. In fact, almost certainly his status was much enhanced as his voice became that of the Allies whereas under

German military rule he would virtually have been ignored.

With the Germans in retreat, he would have inspired, or been privy to, all the covert plans of collecting and hiding foodstuffs and valuables. Organising communes, he took over the least damaged properties to house the homeless; could personally identify remaining skills to try and cope with appalling public emergencies.

Often, as a Company, we were on our own; left to our own devices. In all the flux and uncertainty, survival demanded imagination, off-the-cuff decisions, and action, in which the Burgermeister would be a necessary link. Those demands would reduce him almost to tears!

'Find fifty men to clear this street!'

'Shovels? That's your problem!'

'Three wireless sets, within the hour!'

'Fetch a couple of carpenters!'

'Assemble a hundred men and boys 8 a.m. tomorrow to build a road!

'Six tables. Fifty chairs! We'll collect!'

The Burgermeister would protest but hurry away to please. He was a mine of local information though it had to be diplomatically dragged from him; at times with veiled threats!

AMGOT (Allied Military Government of Occupied Territories) had not been established. Later, when these white-band-around-the-caps did arrive freshly out of Britain, they mostly appeared to be civilians hastily pushed into uniform, nonplussed at being thrust into a wholly unexpected, alien, ravaged, environment.

The O.C. of whichever Company had first moved into a town or village automatically assumed the unofficial tag of 'Town Major'. Having experienced all the initial problems, Units arriving would draw on his knowledge whether a Burgermeister there or not. With any Burgermeister as his channel of communication the Town Major represented Montgomery and therefore the whole British. In fact all ranks were carving impressions which would colour attitudes between the two nations for years to come. These attitudes were strongly influenced by how the Burgermeister was handled.

The profound shock of our very presence in their country must have indicated to all Germans the end was near. In the interests of his own folk the Burgermeister's function was to collaborate. Accustomed to taking orders passed down from one central authority – the Nazi machine – rather than have no orders at all, by nature, those issued by the British were almost welcome!

He certainly helped solve a number of our initial basic problems.

Amongst the many serious demands, that of a lighter kind surprised one Burgermeister! Meeting for the first time, bracing himself for the worst, expecting wholly impossible requisitions, he received a solitary, simple, order.

'Get a man to make two sets of goalposts complete with wooden sockets!' This with a noisy battle raging not far away!

When the end did come, and the Non-Frat Ban finally lifted, a Burgermeister elsewhere would never forget an equally strange request.

'All instruments for a dance band!'

Unexpectedly, they came!

The Company had no difficulty whatever in producing musicians to suit.

Somewhere around Luneberg Heath the largest old German Barracks drill hall was transformed into a 'Mecca Ballroom'.

On the night, the place rapidly filled, leaving hundreds of prettied up frauleins outside, faces pressed against the windows, but, although disappointed, thoroughly enrapt in the bright lights, the jollity and the unscored music! It was later learned an extremely popular film actress amongst them!

That particular event was the nearest thing 'our lot' came to a Victory celebration.

And on this not-to-be-missed special occasion, delightedly, the Burgermeister joined in.

Thanksgiving

It may have been a large church. Maybe a cathedral. Where? Somebody will know.

The occasion, a Second Army representative gathering at the conclusion of the campaign in NW Europe. A massive uniformed congregation, remembering and giving thanks.

Every Corps. Every Division. Every Brigade, Group, Battalion. And even down to Company level. Such a tremendous array of shoulder titles and flashes in evidence! The blue and white shield of the Second Army the common denominator.

Many men and women who, unless compulsorily obliged, would not normally attend a church service had competed to be present, many having travelled considerable distances. Proud and privileged to be taking part in this unique, poignant, yet happy act of worship.

Never was the silence so meaningful, so moving, for those comrades who made the supreme sacrifice, nor the National Anthem – trumpets sounding – sung with such sincerity.

In the issued small pocket size Service booklet those words under the heading 'Then Shall the Chaplain Say' encapsulated the whole mood, each throat-catching prayer emotionally responded to by all.

> 'As we waited by the coasts of our own land for the order that should send us over the Channel, we dedicated ourselves in the sight of God to the task which had been committed to us. We asked that his presence might be with us, to lead us, and to sustain us in the days that lay ahead. Today we once more stand before God to declare our thanks, in the sight of all men, for all the benefits he has granted us during this great campaign.
>
> We thank thee for the protection afforded us by The Royal Navy. Who brought us safely over the Channel. Who covered our landings. And who, with the Merchant Navy, have brought to us safely all our wants.
>
> And for all those who have laboured so willingly in our Docks and Ports.
>
> For the Royal Air Force, and the Allied Air Forces, who removed from the skies the dangers that threatened us. And for their ground support in battle.

For the Armies of our Allies, who have fought on our flanks, and for the spirit of friendship and co-operation that has existed throughout the Allied Expeditionary Force.

For the troops who have been engaged in maintaining and supplying us while in the Field.

For the men and women who have worked long hours in factories, mines and fields to supply, and keep us supplied, with the wonderful equipment that has made victory possible.

For our families, friends and the whole Country, who by their great confidence have encouraged us through the bitterest days.

For those who have cared for and cheered our wounded. And by their skill and patience have assisted in thy work of mercy.

For those who mourn the loss of loved ones, and who have borne their sacrifices with patience and fortitude.

For our Commanders and leaders, who have guided us unwaveringly and unfalteringly through all our great battles.

For the sense that thou hast been with us in all our dangers, trials and tribulations. And for granting final Victory to the Allies.'

The remarkably well-produced Order of Service booklet would have been kept and treasured by participants – its front cover depicting Corps and Divisional flashes vividly presented in a splendid splash of colour.

A reproduction in black and white cannot do it justice, though, to those who wore them, flashes immediately recognisable.

Most fortunately, at the time, a few of us went into a huddle to combine our knowledge. The scribbled identification against each flash, now, so many years later, makes a useful and comprehensive reminder of all those Second Army formations.

KEY

1. Second Army 2. 8 Corps 3. 1st Corps 4. 12 Corps 5. 30 Corps 6. Airborne 7. 15th Guards Armoured 8. 7th Armoured (Desert Rats) 9. 11th Armoured 10. 3rd Infantry 11. 5th Infantry 12. 59th W.L. Infantry (AGRA) 13. 53rd Welsh 14. 52nd (L) Mountain Infantry 15. 51st Highland 16. 15th Scottish 17. 43rd Wessex Infantry 18. 49th (WR) Infantry 19. 50th Northumberland Infantry 20. 6th (Guards) Tank Brigade 21. 4th Armoured Brigade 22. 8th Armoured Brigade 23. 27th Armoured Brigade (Polish) 24. 115 (Indp) Infantry Brigade 25. 33rd Armoured Brigade 26. 34th Armoured Brigade

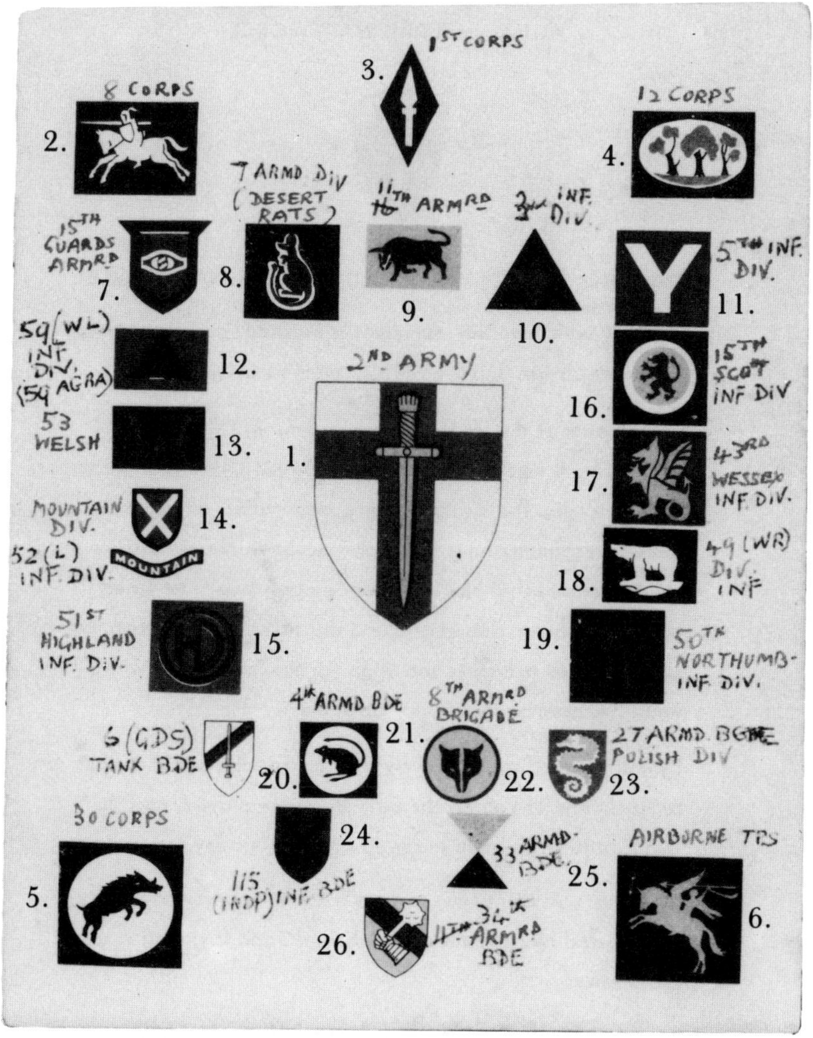

SECOND ARMY FORMATIONS
Campaign in North West Europe
6th June 1944 – 5th May 1945

SUPREME HEADQUARTERS

ALLIED EXPEDITIONARY FORCE

TO ALL MEMBERS OF THE ALLIED EXPEDITIONARY FORCE:

The task which we set ourselves is finished, and the time has come for me to relinquish Combined Command.

In the name of the United States and the British Commonwealth, from whom my authority is derived, I should like to convey to you the gratitude and admiration of our two nations for the manner in which you have responded to every demand that has been made upon you. At times, conditions have been hard and the tasks to be performed arduous. No praise is too high for the manner in which you have surmounted every obstacle.

I should like, also, to add my own personal word of thanks to each one of you for the part you have played, and the contribution you have made to our joint victory.

Now that you are about to pass to other spheres of activity, I say Good-bye to you and wish you Good Luck and God-Speed.

Vodka

Feeding of the civil population was giving headaches.

Montgomery had issued an instruction forbidding any further military requisitioning of farm produce.

Within twenty-four hours commotion and anxious voices outside; and a local farmer plus family were ushered in. Despite the announcement, the farm had been visited by 'Ruskies' – Russian soldiers – and amongst other possessions a pig had been carried off. Please would the British do something about the Russians?

'We'll be meeting them tonight and endeavour to see it won't happen again' the farmer was assured.

The Russians had scant regard for Montgomery and could not understand his authority. They did things their own way. Often in a really big way.

Like the Russian Victory Dinner in Wolfsburg!

That evening, the Town's Intelligence officer, fluent Russian-speaking, led the British contingent of three. In the crisp chill we drove over in an open kübelwagen.

Met by those with whom we were in daily contact, introductions to representatives of all nations were hilarious. Greetings in crude German, the loud attempts to understand each other – and quickly – usually finished up in gales of laughter. It was Babylon! Wine flowed freely. Uninhibited high spirits took over within minutes.

The hall was crowded. Judging by the seating arrangements maybe a couple of hundred had been invited but twice that number appeared to be milling around. Waiters and watiresses pirouetted with trays full of bottles. In no time at all everybody was thoroughly merry.

Uproarious swapping of experiences dropped to a respectful hush as a VIP High Command party entered.

A married Russian officer couple known to us stood nearby. Frequently we had remarked on the total improbability of such a partnership serving in the same unit in the British Army.

Fussed around by flunkeys the gaggle of VIP's held centre stage, when suddenly an astonishing incident made one wonder whether we British would ever possibly understand the Russians!

The Red Tab who appeared the most dominant promptly pointed to the female of the Russian couple. Momentarily hesitant, yet without comment, she left the crowd and disappeared with him. Puzzled 'Vies?' and 'Warums?' addressed to the ashen-faced husband produced nothing. Others were more forthcoming. This was not at all unusual. Sex was an accepted, undeniable privilege of top Russian rank. In disbelief, we suggested the Marshal, or whatever rank he was, must have been wildly drunk?

'If that had been Montgomery himself he'd have found his face smashed in!' I found myself saying.

No, No, the shaken husband explained, with any protest or resistance they would never see each other again . . . ever! They were re-united some little time later. I swear before I'd finished the first drink!

Outnumbered three to one by the caterers, guests were piloted to seats at tables groaning with a gargantuan array which would have done justice to any Mansion House function.

And suddenly, there it was! A whole pig's head! Strategically set on a centre table abutting on to the top table. Quite impossible to forget the morning's promise to the farmer! The thing was within a few feet, its ugly face, wide mouthed, laughing, almost mockingly posing the question 'Who the hell is Montgomery?'!

Huge consignments of vokda, 'the very best' it was boasted, had been flown in direct from Moscow. Etiquette, I was aware, demanded the correct way of sinking this national poor opposite to Scotland's whisky was with one quick thrust to the back of the throat.

Over both shoulders flunkeys hovered, serving hors-deuvre, and re-filling glasses as toasts were launched thick and fast.

'To Generalissimo Josef Stalin!'

'To the President United States!'

'To the King of England!'

'To Churchill!'

'To General Eisenhower!'

'To the Red Army!'

'To the Russian Air Force!'

'To the Russian Navy'

Individually by name so it went on. Other Armies, other Navies, other Air Forces, other Allied personalities! With each toast glasses magically re-filled!

Standing up, woomph! Sitting down. Standing up, woomph! The toasts were endless.

The hors-deuvre remained untasted.

The head thumped alarmingly!

Much be-ribboned hierarchy, faces, strange mixtures of uniforms, bobbled in weird confusion! Ceiling and walls swirled, tilted and danced! The mass of food, particularly that hog's head, leaped and circled around! Peculiarly, voices seemed far far away!

Vodka had hit an empty stomach!

'Intelligence' had been seated some three or four places away. Difficult to focus, impossible to identify him, an alarmed warning shout went into his general direction.

'I'm going! It's up to my eyes!'

Amongst the jumble of foreign tongues a faint English response registered.

'Excuse yourself! I'll explain you've overworked!'

• • •

Five hours later, out in the cold night air, we clambered into the kübelwagen. I remember it well. The trip in silence.

On arrival at the Gasthaus, our quarters, came the awful realisation.

Five lost hours of my life!

Appalled, appealingly, I pressed 'Intelligence' for an exposé.

It sounded genuine enough.

'Well' he said 'You didn't just excuse yourself. Stood up and demanded silence! Interrupted top brass! I had to translate! You made a speech! Roars of applause! Went on about a pig! Pig Hitler! How every person present had helped put his head on a dish! They lapped it up! Cheered! Wanted you to go on. You stood to attention, bowed deeply all round and marched off like a bloody guardsman!'

'Is that all?' I pleaded.

'Yep! And you did pause splendidly for me to translate!'

'But five hours. Five whole hours! What was I doing for five hours?'

'Well, each time we came in to ease springs you were in the same place, gripping the washbasin, staring into the mirror, chastising yourself!'

'How do you mean? What was I saying?'

'Over and over again the same thing!'

'What?'

'You FOOL! You BLOODY fool!'

Of course experience is the best teacher.

How could I possibly know those Russians had perfected the art of emptying vodka between their legs on to the carpet as they sat down after each toast?

Mentioned in Despatches

Acting rank, as you the reader may well have cause to rue, sometimes came suddenly, and just as suddenly went! Occasionally with appropriate pay, more frequently not so!

The Skipper having been posted away, quite happily I'd slotted into the acting job.

A DR had delivered a field message.

Faced with a decision to make, the O.C. 'Griggo' always had the same communicative habit. He would guffaw loudly and await the expected query.

'What's it this time?'

'Company mentioned in despatches! Four to award!'

'Four? That's awkward!'

'Yep! Let's mull it over. Have a chat tonight!'

The matter remained undiscussed until turning in time.

Many an OC would have promptly grabbed one for himself.

Not Griggo!

We shared a tent.

Four cases of individual oustanding conduct in the field would have been difficult to assess, and any such favoured selection inevitably contentious.

'Suggest Major, with great respect for your own service, one, the Sarntmajor, two, the chief cook, three, the most cheerful man, and four, the most popular footballer!' I ventured.

'Snap! Thinking on much the same lines!' nodded Griggo.

So it was!

With the overwhelming approval of the whole outfit the names of four surprised representatives were declared, who duly became entitled to wear that prized oak leaf addition to the France & Germany Star ribbon.

No acts of bravery!

Just four good practical reasons why we believed our Company to be efficient, and, in military interpretation of the term, happy!

And no attempt was made to query the particular incident which prompted official recognition.

Almost certainly everybody would have opted for some OTHER occasion!

Souvenir

May 1945. Under canvas. Germany.

Victory, and the Company's future uncertain.

If returned to the UK the PRI Fund would be claimed as the property of the War Office. To avoid such confiscation would it not be sensible to use the cash, or part of it, on some kind of memento?

A quickly scribbled outline of Company history emerged, gleaned from Reg the Company Clerk and others who had been founder members.

A search enabled a full record of all who had at any time served. In an appendix these names would be listed alphabetically. Wherever they might be, each bod would get a copy of the memento envisaged.

It would also carry a decorative bow in the red and green ribbon of the Corps.

To our delight, a professional artist discovered amongst the thousands of Polish Displaced Persons, designed a suitably attractive coloured front cover.

The booklet would include a rough sketch map showing the Company's peregrinations with the B.L.A.

Not over-ambitious, a draft of a simple souvenir was completed. This would go with me on the first home Leave.

Friendly Woolwich Printers in due course were entrusted to parcel up and send the consignment of three hundred copies direct to Germany.

Placenames shown on that map will ring many a bell! Reminders not only of the bitter and grim, but also those happy 'Cigarette for Papa' glorious days of liberation!

One hopes all listed on that Roll actually DID receive a copy – a reminder of ordinary Support Troop days when the vast majority would only be distinguished by Number, Rank and Name.

1940
1943
LABOR OMNIA VINCIT
Souvenir
126 Company
Pioneer Corps
1941
1944
Presented to :-
Lieut. W. Jardine
1942
126
1945

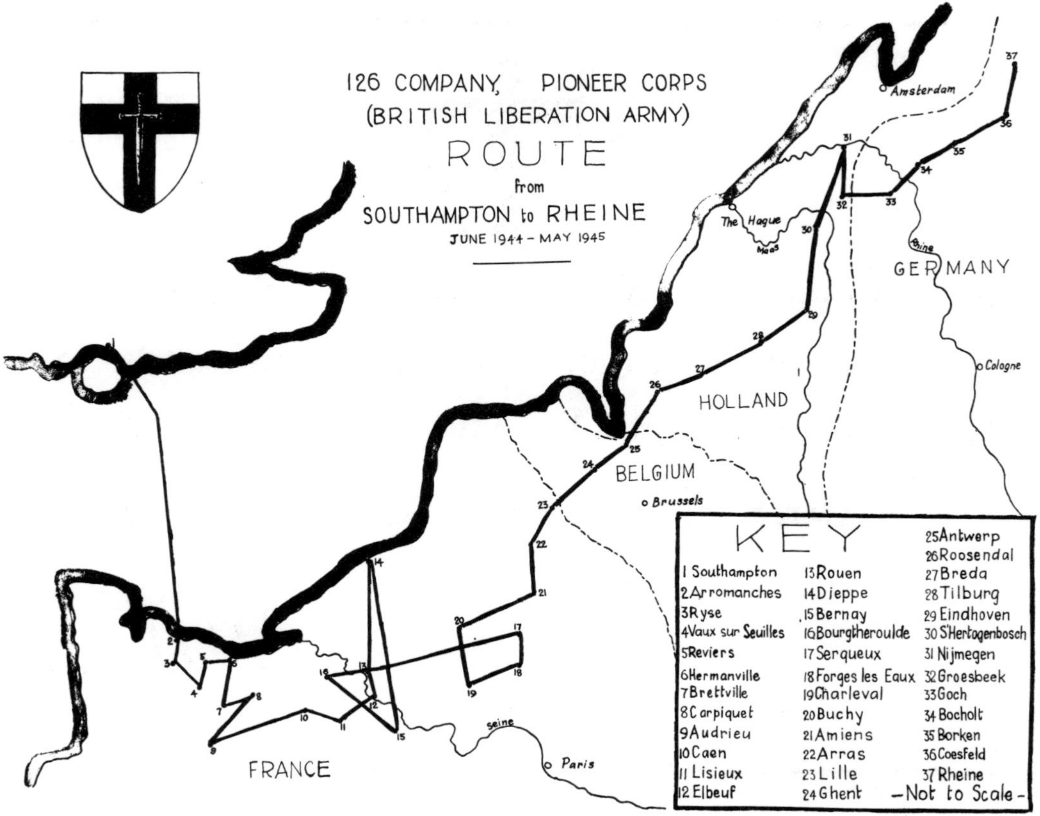
126 COMPANY, PIONEER CORPS
(BRITISH LIBERATION ARMY)
ROUTE
from
SOUTHAMPTON to RHEINE
JUNE 1944 – MAY 1945
FRANCE
BELGIUM
HOLLAND
GERMANY
Amsterdam
The Hague
Maas
Rhine
Cologne
Brussels
Seine
Paris
KEY
1 Southampton
2 Arromanches
3 Ryse
4 Vaux sur Seuilles
5 Reviers
6 Hermanville
7 Brettville
8 Carpiquet
9 Audrieu
10 Caen
11 Lisieux
12 Elbeuf
13 Rouen
14 Dieppe
15 Bernay
16 Bourgtheroulde
17 Serqueux
18 Forges les Eaux
19 Charleval
20 Buchy
21 Amiens
22 Arras
23 Lille
24 Ghent
25 Antwerp
26 Roosendal
27 Breda
28 Tilburg
29 Eindhoven
30 S'Hertogenbosch
31 Nijmegen
32 Groesbeek
33 Goch
34 Bocholt
35 Borken
36 Coesfeld
37 Rheine
– Not to Scale –

As Commander of the Second Army I say to every man under my command and to all ranks of 83 Gp R.A.F. who have supported us

THANK YOU AND WELL DONE

M. C. Dempsey
Lt. General

May 1945

'Small Wonder'

Strangely, the concrete built town, streets built crosswise, American fashion, was not on official maps!

One of the largest Displaced Persons Camps was understood to be at Hesslingen, between Brunswick and Hanover. Arriving there and seeking out the Burgermeister, most surprisingly he produced a map showing the village of that name but surrounded by a whole new town. Dotted lines indicated future proposed development. This 'Stadtplan' declared the town to be Der Stadt Des KDF-Wagens. The KDF was of course 'Kraft-De-Freude', Strength Through Joy, the movement headed by that arch Nazi, Robert Ley. Hesslingen had literally been absorbed and the town was now known as Wolfsburg.

Here was The Volkswagen Motor Works. The name crudely sign-written above the entrance gates.

Birthplace of the ugly, noisy, ubiquitous 'Beetle'!

The town, dull and bleak, with its plain concrete constructions two or three floors high had been specifically designed to meet the needs of factory workers, here and there streets petering out leading nowhere, all building work having abruptly stopped.

Before the war, newspapers and the media had enlightened us on Hitler's pet project 'The People's car'; of his obsession to provide every German family with an automobile. His involvement with the car industry was well known.

We were to learn that even after war broke out he insisted on the scheme going ahead. His insistence had been shortlived. The factory switched to producing the kübelwagen – the open high-chassis dodgem-type steel jeep which helped to motorise the German infantry.

To the best of our knowledge only three of these remained mobile in the town, and had of course been taken over. An initial fourth share in one, though useful, proved frustratingly inconvenient!

Hostilities had now finished.

Hitherto accustomed to all ranks more or less sharing the same close quarters, most peculiarly OC's and 2 i/c's of all Units based locally were billetted together in a Guesthouse. Although purely living quarters this central Mess served as a loosely contrived Sub-Command HQ. A nerve centre, a controlling fulcrum, where informal off-duty chats gelled and co-ordinated all that was going on in the area. Actual duties and purpose of some of the residents remained extremely vague. As the only one below the rank of Captain my presence seemed odd.

The Guesthouse had all the trimmings of a three-star hotel.

It had been built for VIP visitors to the Motor Works. Hitler, Goering, Goebbels, Ribbentrop, Ley, Hess, Himmler and others in the Nazi hierarchy stayed here regularly in the heady days.

When taken over by the Americans the house staff had remained on and continued to be employed, hence batmen, relieved of normal chores settled for the role of 'valet' only!

Conducted by one of the German housemaids to the room allocated me, having no choice in the matter, it was unnerving to find this very large, very splendid! Most decidedly puzzling! It was apparent senior ranks had opted for much less opulent rooms. Why should this be so? Why had such a special room been avoided? The housemaid provided enlightenment. It had been kept, hitherto, exclusively for Hitler's personal use on his frequent visits! Hell! It was late. Protest would be useless. There was no option but to get into that bed! Fortunately, after an extremely tiring day sleep came quickly, and to the breakfast-time ribbings, No, I was not particularly proud of the doubtful 'honour', and No, had not been troubled by anything paranormal! No ghosts walking!

Events were to show one's duties carried considerable licence over and above normal Company involvement. Denied a Royal Engineers commission with no vacancies during the 'phoney War', that Movement Control connection had obviously been sussed out! Clearly, the expectation was that whatever problems existed or whatever assistance called for movements-wise in the town there must needs be a catalyst.

Wolfsburg was becoming an important staging post. From Schleswig Holstein and Heligoland, particularly, a vast exodus was under way. Streams of traffic, of all Services and nationalities were passing through. Amusingly, many in peculiar colourful uniforms wholly unrecognised as friend or foe!

To cater for these travellers Reception points, feeding and sleeping stations, vehicle repair centre and all associated arrangements began to take shape. Extra cooks, still more cooking equipment, extra beds and bedding somehow scraped together. It became a non-stop, exhilarating business. A front room set up at Company HQ blossomed as the town's Emergency Office.

Vested with all keys to the town, these occupied a whole room elsewhere in the old official Administrative building, each key tabbed, hanging uniformly on all four walls, and supervised by 'the key frau'.

Her knowledge of buildings in the town encyclopaedic she had been happy to have been kept on, uncomplainingly turning out any time during the day or night as circumstances dictated.

Beyond the old Hesslingen village end of the town stretched a vast area of hutments. Previously a German Army Camp, these now occupied by thousands upon thousands of DP's. Before dispersal started of every nationality – Russians, Poles, French, Latvian, Lithuanian, Czechs, Danish, Swiss, Swedes, Norwegians, Italians, Hungarians, Belgians, Dutch, Estonians and many Stateless. Others having been fairly promptly cleared, the vast Russian and Polish Camps remained, overcrowded with ragged humanity herded together squalidly. Such a hotch potch of bodies; here and there rough hessian or old clothing strung up contriving a modicum of family privacy.

These DPs patiently awaited sorting out and transporting away. The Company's special task was to supervise and feed this multitude. Hundreds of dixies of hot soup would regularly be distributed.

Pioneers toiled cheerfully in the shocking, scruffy, and unhealthy surroundings. A labour of mercy, and often the milk of human kindness so truly touching to witness! Language no barrier, those DP's were contantly expressing appreciation; not just for the food.

One of the CSM's special responsibilities was the weeding out of imposters – branded SS men posing as DP's. These would be taken to the local Civil Gaol. Protocol perhaps, not being in military uniform. But we didn't ask questions. What an incongruous performance that was! Passage-ways narrow and twisting, the old gaoler led the way, followed by handing-over officer, prisoners, and bringing up the rear, the armed guard: the last mentioned frequently out of sight. A comic and bizarre routine! I've often wondered whether the old gaoler kept those SS men under lock and key for long!

In the Polish DP Camp, organisation and communication became simpler by the discovery of a shy, timid, Pole who could speak some English – promptly recruited as unofficial interpreter and rewarded with perks. His finding proved useful. At our level the affairs of Poland were a complete mystery. Politicians had ordered a Plebiscite. A mass of papers arrived, printed in Polish. We gathered the purpose was for each individual DP to declare past records and loyalties and to establish future aspirations – who wanted to return home and who didn't . . . which was to spark off much unrest and argument. Having no idea of the implications of the Potsdam Agreement which followed the meeting of Stalin, Roosevelt and Churchill, we ourselves were working in the dark.

Then came somebody's blunder!

The powers-that-be, expecting trouble, deemed it politic to instal Polish *irregular* troops into the Camp, presumably on the grounds of neutrality. Why the much respected Polish regular forces were not drawn upon seemed to us a complete mystery! And why it was felt resident British troops could not ensure complete neutrality an even bigger mystery!

In fact tension was exacerbated.

Within days, without warning, a tremendous cacophony of machine gun and rifle fire echoed from the direction of the Polish Camp. The office door crashed open. In flew our friend the interpreter screaming for protection. 'The troops' had tried to kill him.

Immediately calling the guard out, a truckload careered to the Camp. Thousands of confused, terrified, DP's blocked the way!

'Foot down hard!'

It was the only chance. The driver responded. Horn blowing, headlights flashing, somehow the crowd scattered as the vehicle hurtled towards the sound of fresh bursts of gunfire. Quite obviously the Polish Irregulars had gone berserk!

Seeing the lorry bearing down on them, all firing ceased. The perpetrators made for their hut, pursued by an armed posse of Pioneers in full war cry. The sight of a British officer's uniform and menacing revolver had an immediate, magical, effect! Guns ordered to be dropped, the patently drunk Polish guard mob quickly obeyed, surrounded as they were by Pioneers threatening to blow some heads off! An illicit still continued to bubble! The contraption, wrecked by rifle butt swipes, was swept on to the lorry together with all the hut's contents.

To the relief of the DP's the Irregulars were quickly marched off and incarcerated.

The DP's drifted away and the camp resumed normal lassitude. (The plebiscite was conducted without incident by Pioneers a few days later.)

But that evening a highly amused Colonel beckoned over and greeted one subaltern.

'Bloody madman! Endangering British lives! What you don't know is that I'd already planned the closedown of that Polish armed lot! If you'd left 'em alone might have killed each other off and saved us some bother! You'll have a quieter day tomorrow – I want you to do something for me!' Which aroused curiosity.

• • •

The mission, to report in a preliminary manner whether or not the Volkswagen Works merited repair.

The kübelwagen was headed into the desolation.

Not even a guard placed on the site, the ruins had been a complete irrelevance. Comprehensively, and for the record, most accurately bombed by the RAF and USAF, I reckoned to give no more than an hour on this tour of inspection. That would be ample. I was anxious to be away on more immediate and important matters! Driving where the vehicle would go, scrambling to vantage points, scribbling notes and sketches, this was something for the future!

Of some seven main complexes it appeared only two might conceivably be reconstructed. In the tangle of rubble and steel it was everywhere impossible to define any machinery at all. Incidentally, it was much later one learned 3,500 DP's had been forced, in 12-hour shifts, into the making of the first of those unwelcome V1 'doodlebugs' here.

A quick gut conclusion was to bulldoze the lot, letting hardcore go for essential road construction so that when peace came architects could start from scratch with a clean uncluttered site.

The town itself virtually unscathed, some day, when re-populated, industrial capacity and jobs would be essential. Tacit, this went into the report.

Shortly afterwards a REME officer, delegated by the War Office, joined us. His brief, to make an official report. Was it a Major Hirst? Together, in the kübelwagen, we toured the ruined Works.

Now, on the table, is the map handed to me by the Burgermeister, his house marked in pencil. Some present day burghers would be amazed to see it.

Wolfsburg is a large city.

The dreaded V1 a fading memory.

The kübelwagen no doubt a museum piece.

But EVERYBODY knows about the VW BEETLE!

Hitler couldn't conquer the world, but amazingly his dream car 'The Small Wonder' DID!

The Last Trainload

'Katishka' was the name we gave her. It sounded right, though she always found it amusing. Some-one with a knowledge of Russian may explain why.

Small, slim, almost fragile, she appeared much too petit for the job, but clearly she was most competent in organising and supervising Russian DP's scheduled to travel homewards.

When trainloads were laid on she could be seen either in the depressing conditions of the DP camp earnestly discussing matters of detail with those truly wretched victims, or already down at the Station, shepherding, consoling, assisting, and generally directing the unfortunates into large covered trucks.

Without official instruction or design it became customary for Katishka to give the nod when all were aboard.

Never at any time did she go out of her way to consult, or to seek help, or to report. It was accepted she would have to be found: unthinkable the train should depart without her approval.

She wore no uniform. No badge of office. Head never covered, her jet black hair streamed in the wind and rain: her dress always the same - simple and sombre, befitting the appallingly sad circumstances. She went about her ministrations quietly and unwaveringly.

Who she was, where she came from, where she operated at other times, where she domiciled when in Wolfsburg, no-one knew, nor would dream of asking. Always she departed with each trainload.

In later days Russian military personnel became much in evidence but the traditional reference to Katishka remained sacrosanct. Young and unofficial though she was, she alone had the experience and our respect. She, and we, carried on almost as if the increasing number of Russian troops had gone unnoticed. She appeared to tolerate their presence almost with disdain. Katishka continued her solo work exactly as before. Those of us involved undeviatingly regarded her as the real authority.

On these departures the large goods wagons were unfailingly decorated with a mass of greenery artistically arranged around huge colourful head and shoulder impressions of Stalin and wellknown Russian hero Generals, Rossokovsky, Zhukov and others, all under the critical eye of Katishka.

Before the first homegoing DP's began to arrive Katishka could be spotted nipping from wagon to wagon examining interiors, satisfying herself on the cleanliness of floors.

Many leaving DP Camp behind did so without knowing what the fate had been of spouses; whole families. Release, which should have been a joyful occasion, sad with forebodings and fear. This young girl raised the spirits of them all.

Katishka certainly was a mystery girl. And remained so!

On a particular normal dispersal morning Pioneers had risen at a customary early hour to prepare and distribute the usual soup. Though some thousands of Russian DP's still encamped, nobody had taken the trouble to let it be known this trainload would be the final one destined to travel over the military demarcation line into what was called 'Little Russia'! Ours not to reason why!

Others however did not regard it as a routine day. Kitted out in khaki, a young female press reporter approached, looking for a story. Fleet Street knew more about what was going on than we did! Two Russian officers were urged to look after her.

Initially hidden from view by the stationary train a hundred-piece Russian military band had assembled. With first DP arrivals the blasting of stirring marches and folk tunes hit the quiet morning air.

Entertainers were arriving too! Dancers, acrobats, jugglers, and a massive mixed choir. This was far from being a normal day. It was celebration on a grand scale! Brightly coloured costumes contrasted sharply with the DP's drab clothing.

Entrainment completed; the entertainment, the subdued hand-clapping, ceased. Ostentatiously, high ranking Russian officers were being ushered to a temporarily erected dais.

Train departure time imminent, clearly the usual walk to find Katishka would have to wait!

The two Russians charged with looking after the English press reporter returned with an invitation, a personal invitation, to join the VIP's.

Obviously declined. This was exclusively a Russian affair!.

Orders barked out. Extra loudly the band launched into what must have been some meaningful national tune. Russian military jumped to attention and the salute. Likewise, as etiquette demanded, one train i/c.

Pressmen and photographers chasing about, explaining there would be a further salute.

'The event would appear in Pravda... Isvestia.. Would the British-man move nearer the main party?'.

An almightly patriotic crescendo sounded the programme's end.

Train departure considerably overdue, to walk along the full length of the platform it would be necessary to pass in front of, and disregard, the important hierarchy. High command quite powerless. Only one person could make that train move!

She was up near the engine; lightly, unobtrusively, purposefully, going about her business, flitting from truck to truck, rearranging greenery in her stride. One wondered why she had not been invited to the ceremonial business. Perhaps she had.

'Katishka! Go? Go? Go?'

She nodded her head without a flicker of a smile or having been remotely aware of the big show.

Signal given to engine driver by the stand-in Movements Officer, his arm remained aloft in a final farewell wave as the last trainload of DP's inched out. Within minutes it would cross the military demarcation line which in due course was to so dramatically separate and wall apart the two Germanies.

As usual, 'Katishka' went.

We never saw her again.

• • •

Years later, the British Newspaper Library provided a photostat page of The Daily Herald containing a report written by Mea Allan - the young female reporter.

The Russian papers would have been interesting.

Katishka. Did she ever disclose her DP role and experiences? Now she will be old and wrinkled, perhaps even more slight of build; but remembering those tragic times maybe, just maybe, she recalls working in the path of duty with a British serviceman whose rank and name she neither knew nor wished to know, but who, language no barrier, accorded her respect and courtesy so abyssmally absent from her own military compatriots.

Old and wrinkled? Oh No! With not a little admiration I choose to remember Katishka as a vibrantly young Russian mystery girl of boundless energy and gifted with truly exceptional compassion.

The Missing Day

Germany. September 1945.

VE Day, VJ Day, had come and gone.

All impetus, endeavour and dedication having fizzled out Second Army Troops had little enthusiasm for the mundane daily life.

There had been a minimum of Victory jubilation. In fact all had been asked, nay instructed, to go about as unsmilingly as possible!

Supply work and repairs to vital communications continued apace, aided by German Labour Companies which had been formed. A brief attachment to one of these outfits was more than enough! Utterly boring, they ran themselves with the most extraordinary thoroughness and iron discipline - a British presence merely token!

What became known as The Khaki Election had also come and gone, the procedure for which now quite forgotten, though not the crude notice 'Vote Labour - or I'll break your neck!' displayed before democractic neutrality demanded its removal. Good old Sarntmajor. He always was over-enthusiastic!

For many, days in Germany were numbered.

'Surplus to Requirements' - few resented being so described - received the expected orders for a return to the UK. The prospect of disembarkation privilege leave loomed large!

A big mixed trainful, including our Company, was scheduled to depart from Hanover 08.00 hrs 30th September. Nominated as Train Co-ordinator, it was apparent Movements, again, remembered an old boy!

Individuals and formations, of all Services, would travel light. Personal kit only. Transport, tentage, ammo, stores of every description including the peculiar paraphernalia accumulated by any unit, all would be handed in and left behind.

'We're NOT parting with the dixies!' declared the Major most emphatically. He was remembering having been stranded for a whole day in the Arnhem area and the failure of the promised ration truck to turn up!

Hardly surprising therefore, those dixies were placed in the goods van, totally unobserved.

The Station forecourt a hive of activity, vehicles from a wide area disgorged personnel of all ranks, all Services.

Runners reported Units had boarded; a walk along the platform confirmed named VIP's were seated; a nod to the German driver and, precisely to time, the train pulled out.

Hanover had taken a hammering, but on reaching Osnabruck, which the line skirted, the train chugged past the most ghastly devastation. To men standing at windows, watching, it appeared most of the City had been flattened. This would remain, indelibly impressed on the memory, as the last recollection of service in Germany.

Few wanted to talk. Those who did reflected on arrival in the UK. To which part of the UK would the unit be posted? Would it be disbanded? How would Leave be organised? Would it materialise? Conjecture. Speculation. Hope. A complete absence of jollity and boisterousness.

The engine too had put in some service. Old, much travelled, pulling such a large number of carriages, progress was slow. Inevitably, there were unscheduled halts. As the day wore on and the sunshine intensified, men were sweltering in the cramped compartments, taking turns at leaning out to catch a possible cooling draught of air.

The enforced stops became irritatingly regular.

In the intense heat, anticipating one breakdown would allow time, troops could be seen leaving the train, heading across fields to remote houses, desperate for a drink of water - scorning the long accepted practice of only imbibing water chemically treated by the Horrocks pack. Of these de-hydrated searchers those who failed to rejoin the train would contrive their own onward passage and explain their own absence if unlucky.

The stifling heat became almost intolerable.

Food and drink had been scheduled at a large specially constructed Transit Camp strategically sited miles from anywhere. For first glimpse of that oasis bodies crowded round the windows. Moisture, a small wet, would never be so welcome!

Strangely, the platform was empty, and even more strangely the whole Camp looked deserted.

Shinning over locked gates a shouting search party failed to find anybody. And no food. No stores. Nothing! Water the extreme urgency, all taps were frantically turned on. Not a trickle!

Stop cocks located and freed, the water supply had been very effectively, totally, cut off!

Telephones were tried. All dead.

The awful news travelled like wildfire.

There had been one ghastly, unbelieveable, error of planning . . . AND NO WATER !!

Crisis? This was more than a crisis!

Time for top-level handling, and decision! Particularly as men were collapsing, and others scrambling to open large packs to extract prized bottles of liqueur preciously hoarded for loved ones back home - Benedictine, Vieille Curé, Cointreau!

Confronting the most senior officer on board, stricken and sick he pleaded to be left alone!

Senior rank having fudged, the issue was clear. The almighty problem rested with the train co-ordinator!

Schweik! What would Schweik have done? Think!

Definitely no water to be had in the Camp. But there WAS water.

HOT water! IN THE ENGINE!!

Dixies were aboard. Lashings of tea!

If something wasn't done quickly frenzied men could go bezerk: might wreck the train!

A hurried conference and the proposition -cum-instruction to put to the engine crew was being framed. 'Wir musst vasser von ihren zug haben!' - yes, they would understand that. But when put to the crew it was met with hurt protest.

'Please! Speak English. We're Dutch!'.

Of course, the crew always changed at the border!

Now, more bad news. They had expected to take on a fresh supply of water here for the engine!

Right or wrong the decision was made.

Hurrying for the dixies men lined up at the engine. An overruled driver supervised the extraction of boiling water.

It would take time. Sergeants volunteered to walk the line ahead in the hope of finding a telephone.

The activity triggered off relayed shouts all along the platform.

'Somebody's making a drink! Tea! Tea coming up! Tea!!'.

Mugs immediately fluttered semaphore-wise in their hundreds.

Soon, dozens of dixies full of the reviving char were carried by laughing Pioneers and strategically placed along the platform; others in support brandishing milk and sugar.

'Every man one mugful! No cheating!' Still further excursions up to the engine. Still further dixie deliveries!

'Empty the bloody engine if necessary!' the cry.

'To Hell with the consequences!' heard all round.

This was not the feeding of the five thousand but came perilously near the salvation of almost the two thousand! Temperature in the eighties, parched throats moistened, appreciations were voiced all round.

The senior officer, a Brigadier, had sufficiently recovered. Cap flailing, he clamoured for attention.

'Three cheers for the Pioneers!' he bawled.

The response reflected genuine thanks.

Hanging on to those dixies had been a more than brilliant inspiration!

The Sergeants had returned. Couldn't get to a telephone but civilians had promised to report the train's breakdown.

The disconsolate driver gravely warned of serious trouble. Real danger. So much water had been drawn off didn't think it wise to move any further. The predicament was re-assessed.

Should we sit it out to await the cool of the evening and possible arrival of a replacement engine? Would such delay mean missing the boat and further foul-ups at Ostend? Hanging around would not go down at all well. Right! We would press on regardless. Which did not please the driver.

'Engine could go bang!' he warned.

'Come on! Have a go! Try! Try!' we urged.

'No! Train heavy. Dangerous!'

It was then Schweik recalled a German engine crew's similar resistance. Maybe the same solution might work.

'Please! I come in the cab with you. If trouble we jump out together!'

Counter to all his professional reasoning, but to his eternal credit, the driver agreed.

All aboard, it didn't take long - but of course - for steam to be raised. With a clatter of bumpers the train lurched forward. Painfully slowly, the journey was under way again.

Up front, on the footplate, awaiting disaster, three faces repeatedly looked skywards!

In what seemed an eternity the next station came into view. Having cautiously nursed that old engine, listened to its hiccups, bringing the skill and knowledge of a lifetime to bear, the driver shut everything off. We free-wheeled to the platform.

By improvised means the engine was re-watered.

Had it been seriously damaged? Would it, could it, struggle on to Ostend?

Punctuated by stops, some determined as wise by the driver, many hours overdue, the long journey over, we were in Ostend. We'd made it!

Things were all now in the hands of the RTO.

Walking towards the Station exit we were joined by a Sapper Captain, in civil life he'd been a senior Railway official.

'Confidentially' he murmured 'You know that Continental engine water is dynamite? Engines quite different? No water treatment towers? Ghastly de-scaling chemicals used? Realise you might have poisoned the whole trainload?'

'So you didn't touch the tea?' we challenged.

'No option!' he confessed! 'Took a chance! But tell you what . . . soon as poss I'll be getting a jab to make sure!'.

As for that Transit Camp mystery, much later and only by persistent enquiry through friends, it was discovered the idiot who arranged the train movement actually knew it was due to close down on the last day of the month, but incredibly had forgotten, or perhaps never learnt, the old jingle

'Thirty days hath September,
April, June and November.'

He had wholly worked on there being THIRTY-ONE days in September!

Of such simple ignorance crises are born.

Some mothers do 'ave 'em!

21 ARMY GROUP

PERSONAL MESSAGE FROM THE C-IN-C

(To be read out to all Troops)

1. On this day of victory in Europe I feel I would like to speak to all who have served and fought with me during the last few years. What I have to say is very simple, and quite short.

2. I would ask you all to remember those of our comrades who fell in the struggle. They gave their lives that others might have freedom, and no man can do more than that. I believe that He would say to each one of them:

   "Well done, thou good and faithful servant."

3. And we who remain have seen the thing through to the end; we all have a feeling of great joy and thankfulness that we have been preserved to see this day.

   We must remember to give the praise and thankfulness where it is due:

   "This is the Lord's doing, and it is marvellous in our eyes."

4. In the early days of this war the British Empire stood alone against the combined might of the axis powers. And during those days we suffered some great disasters; but we stood firm: on the defensive, but striking blows where we could. Later we were joined by Russia and America; and from then onwards the end was in no doubt. Let us never forget what we owe to our Russian and American allies; this great allied team has achieved much in war; may it achieve even more in peace.

5. Without doubt, great problems lie ahead; the world will not recover quickly from the upheaval that has taken place; there is much work for each one of us.

   I would say that we must face up to that work with the same fortitude that we faced up to the worst days of this war. It may be that some difficult times lie ahead for our country, and for each one of us personally. If it happens thus, then our discipline will pull us through; but we must remember that the best discipline implies the subordination of self for the benefit of the community.

6. It has been a privilege and an honour to command this great British Empire team in Western Europe. Few commanders can have had such loyal service as you have given me. I thank each one of you from the bottom of my heart.

7. And so let us embark on what lies ahead full of joy and optimism. We have won the German war. Let us now win the peace.

8. Good luck to you all wherever you may be.

B. L. Montgomery

Field-Marshal,
C.-in-C.,
21 Army Group.

Germany,
8 May, 1945.

Cartoon published in THE DAILY DISPATCH *of November 7, 1945.*

Football Strike ? Send for the Pioneers !

BUTTERWORTH

Antwerp wartime Dock Strike experience proved useful during the Merseyside Dock Strike of 1945. Original of this cartoon (which hung at Group HQ) was gifted by Butterworth, who, together with The Marquess of Donegal, Frank Owen, Pat Murphy, and other well-known Fleet Street 'characters', served with author in the early days of the Home Guard at The Royal Dockyard, Woolwich.
(With acknowledgements to Butterworth)

A Brother

The most ordinary service in the most ordinary Unit, be what it may, encouraged a deep belief in the inevitability of whatever will be will be. A firm conviction all had been planned.

Pre-determined.

Goings and comings. Good times, bad times. The right place at the right time; wrong place at the wrong time. Nothing could be done about it.

Such fatalism undoubtedly shaped many who wore uniform. Braced them for whatever lay in store during the rest of their days. Still does I'm sure.

From Germany my Company had been returned to the UK without me. Transferred to another Company not many weeks passed before it too was destined to follow, landing up, in of all places, the old barracks of The Manchester Regiment. The very complex of buildings where my own brother Bob had volunteered on his seventeenth birthday back in 1929! Conscription was unnecessary in those days! Massive unemployment, with hundreds of boys chasing one poorly paid job, filled the ranks.

How strange to be walking, if stutteringly, the very same echoing stone-floored corridors which he, in the full bloom of youth, would have hastened along to the Parade Ground!.

For seven years it had been India, Burma and the Far East for him. Another Number, Rank and Name. At the beginning it was not very long before he'd distinguished himself as an athlete and been withdrawn to become batman to the Colonel, Freyburg by name, a New Zealander, destined to become a General and whose name and record can be found in any good Dictionary of Biographies.

After those seven years, a change of uniform and into the Palestine Police. Another Number and Rank. This at the height of the Arab/Jew conflict when rounding any corner in Jerusalem, Jaffa, and elsewhere, spelt trouble.

In September 1939 he'd debunked. Deserted! Made his way nefariously back to Lancashire to rejoin the old Regiment. Picked up, he'd been shipped back East to continue policing. Wanted to do what he could do best, soldiering, and again repeated the attempt, with the same result; under very close arrest until facing Palestine Police trial.

I have often wondered what sort of job any defending officer could make of that lot!

To kill off any possible third effort the Police authorities must have relented and compromised. Though holding him to obligations, by secondment, allowed him to join the Services. Not the Army, but The Royal Navy.

Given a gunboat, a crew of two, and the freedom of the Sea of Galilee! Chasing arms smugglers sneaking in and out of its small ports. I can well visualize him kitted out in naval whites, cap set at a jaunty Beatty angle, but even the honour of being the first Palestine Policeman ever to be transferred to the Senior Service would have been poor compensation for being kept away from those Manchesters!

Very difficult to explain that ever-increasing pull of 'the old Regiment'.

An important slice of one's life.

A sort of love-hate relationship.

An umbilical cord of ingrained loyalty and allegiance.

Time-served, and the war over, off he went to try Oil in the Persian Gulf. Unable to settle, on to manage a remote maize mill in Southern Rhodesia, where, on a weekly trip by horseback to the nearest town with the takings he'd been ambushed and roughed up.

The lonely life was not for him.

It was back in uniform again: as a guard on East African Railways. Back to 'the boys', and the beer, and the popular sportsman he always was. Though representing 'the Regiment' at every conceivable game possible, taken along for sundowners to Choma Golf Club introduced him to a new challenge! He *was* a natural, and in the first season, Club Champion!

Through all skirmishes, fracas and dangers he emerged unscathed, only to meet his Waterloo in a railway accident! Of course he would have laughed at the irony of that!

He died young. What a full, active, infectiously happy life he enjoyed! It rubbed off everywhere!

I hold his medals.

In reverie, I think of being given more than seventyfive years.

An ever-caring wife. Children. Grandchildren.

Service life tells me it was *all* pre-determined.

Okinawa

Absorbed and preoccupied in the frenzy of ever-changing daily events one enraged Group Colonel had been dismissed from mind, as had the proffered assistance to get those Ruhr coalfields functioning again!

The new Major didn't know me, nor I him.

Urgently calling me into Company office there was a tinge of awe in his voice.

'You've done some VC jobs in your time!'

'Who? Me? What on earth are you talking about?'

'Hadn't realised you were a specialist in Air-strip emergency repair work'.

'What?! Nor me!!'

'Group DR's just been in with this. You're posted'.

He pushed across a Movement Order.

First glance picked out the planning for one's immediate future!

'Token British Task Force...Seconded to USA . . . Airstrips under attack...Okinawa...'.

'Major, this is absolutely crazy. Never been on an airfield, let alone an airstrip!' (I hadn't!).

'Your Colonel friend pulling a fast one?'

'Looks like it!'

'He's determined to get you, dead or alive, isn't he?'

So it was once again off to Overseas Assembly Centre, Prestatyn, and the magic of another fourteen days Embarkation leave. What precious days! Such glorious days! How good to be home - surely something only Service people can *really* understand?

Back at Prestatyn, making a beeline to the Drafts Notice Board how puzzling to find, though much had happened, many drafts notified, nothing at all of personal moment. Chasing to the office, the C.O. agreed my call had supposedly been 'urgent and important'.

'Well' he observed 'Something will turn up soon. Hang around and be our guest! Maybe they've forgotten! You're the only one from the whole Corps for that Task Force and one won't make much difference!'.

How true. How very true!

Another week went by. A most restful week.

Still nothing!

Brother, something's gone wrong, that's for sure: but what? Long ago one learned never to be really surprised - uncertainties of Service life the norm.

At last it came! My Number, Rank and Name pinned up there! What? Impossible!

'To proceed on fourteen days leave - Embarkation delayed'

Delayed? They could say that again! But surely not another lot of Leave? Got to be some mistake! I'd nip into the Colonel's den: he'd sort things out.

'Don't breathe a word' he murmured confidentially 'but the whole of that Task Force quite possibly could be abandoned. There's a whisper around that the Japs are thinking of packing up!'

'Must have heard Schweik was coming!'

'Schweik? Who the hell is Schweik?' queried a very puzzled C.O. 'Now get off home again and enjoy yourself!'.

• • •

Tearful goodbyes still fresh in the memory, a most surprised wife and small son welcomed me back.

Still limping, the unexpected continuous rest from active duty had been a godsend and I felt positively cheerful; almost grateful to those Japs; but the double Embarkation leave was soon over.

Back to Prestatyn, a visit to the Drafts Notice Board was the obvious first priority.

Standing there, studying the detail, alone, was a Colonel. Immediately recognisable! From the old Group in Germany. The very Colonel who wished me on some blistering airstrip in Okinawa!

'Hello Colonel!'.

White, tight-lipped, he looked completely shocked.

'What brings you here Colonel?'

Without answer, he turned and hurried away.

Scanning the notice board for explanation, there it was! A draft listed for far distant Singapore: he as Conducting Officer in charge!

Of my fate, nothing. But what profound relief my name was not amongst those to accompany him!

As a familiar visitor to Depot Office there was little difficulty in reaching the inner sanctum to quiz a much more humane Colonel.

'Hello there' came a cheerful greeting 'Had a good Leave? Come and sit down. Know what? You're a very lucky chap - you're for Kenya! Marvellous! Been there! And Oh Yes! I was right about that Jap rumour. It's all off! But a bit of advice - Try and forget about witch-hunts and personal vendettas. These things do tend to get around! Matter of fact your friend is here!'

'Thanks a lot, Sir! And yes, I've seen him'.

'He's for Singapore! Keep this to yourself - they couldn't make it Okinawa!' confided the Colonel!

Who said Army brass was full of dunderheads?

• • •

About to climb up the gangway of the troopship bound for Mombasa, above the hubbub of dockside activity somebody was shouting my name.

It was a Movement Control old buddy of Weavers Down Sapper training days, now a Corporal, vigorously waving some letters.

'Sorting mail this morning, grabbed these! Explained why I'd deliver 'em personally!'

Ships that pass in the night! How great to see a familiar face! Reminisced on the early days which seemed an eternity ago.

Of the two letters one, from my wife, was slipped into a pocket for later savouring at leisure.

Opening the other, it was a friendly scribbled note from a Company Commander I'd been with in Germany. Now back in the UK he'd somehow learned of my sailing from Southampton. It simply said 'Thought you'd be interested in having this. It's been following you round Germany. Good Luck! HFH'.

The enclosure was a tattered, very dirty, brown envelope covered with a multitude of re-directions, some in ink, some in pencil, many faint, some indecipherable. Badly crumpled, it had at some time been very wet. Fragile, it needed to be most gently opened, and inside, a Field Message! Dating back many weeks, though having gone through so many hands, clearly readable:

> URGENT & IMPORTANT. Report IMMEDIATELY to Commanding Officer, Coal Commission ESSEN. Location Map Reference.. EXTREMELY URGENT...repeat EXTREMELY URGENT.

'Know what, pal, this could have changed the whole of my life!'

'But not for the better?' suggested the Corporal.

Scruffing the relic into a pocket, we said our goodbyes, and I went aboard, ready for East Africa.

That Field Message was too late. So too was the call of Okinawa!

Troopship

What a mixed bag from all Services crowded on to the troopship 'Stratheden' bound for east of Suez, where, until he's been, man hasn't lived! So they say!

The triumph of intricate planning allowing exercise for all on limited deckspace; inter-regimental rivalry exploding in a boxing ring erected aft; tannoy announcements of 'Man Overboard' (consternation dissolving into mirth when the star of the drama discovered in Sick Bay!), sweepstakes guessing the ship's daily mileage, winner's cash haul fabulous; cramped living quarters accepted as the norm.

Reaching Port Said, flurries of Customs, Port, Naval, Immigration and Military small craft; graceful cavortings of fat sharks; buzzing human sharks in the shape of 'bum boys' nudging giftladen craft with their 'How moosh ye geeve Mr. Mactaveesh?' and flinging lines to decks high above for items to be hauled up, examined, and payment sent back; native youngsters precariously perched on gigantic oil pipes, skilfully, uncannily, throwing oranges into raised hands, and diving to retrieve coinage not so cleverly returned; kitbags dumped higgledy-piggledy overside into barges; disembarking Service people beetling across a pontoon jetty.

Going ashore verboten for all others!

In translucent morning brilliance a whole fishing fleet of dhows on the move.

So were we.

On through the Canal and its Bitter Lakes, to Tewfik.

Hot days soaking up the sun.

Card games and sessions of 'Housey-Housey', the only legitimized gambling, whiling away the evenings.

Eventually, that wonderful tropical vista of the African coastline before docking at Kilindini, port of Mombasa, to be greeted, amongst others, by grinning red-fezzed native Military Police wearing the most enormous boots ever! (Silly how such trifles stick in the mind!).

Seventeen days out of the UK and a calculated six thousand one hundred and thirty one miles at sea, with still something like four hundred ahead by rail to Nairobi.

A long, long way from home. Already thinking of the return journey and Civvie Street! Always wishing time and one's young life away! Always!

That's how it was.

The Baggage Wallah

At Kilindini the troopship had landed a small draft en route to Ruiru.

The baggage-detailed man let it be known all personal heavy gear had been seen out of the hold and loaded on to the train at Mombasa Station, with which news all could relax.

The humidity was stifling.

The engine refused to start.

Hours passed.

Impatiently waiting about in the choking, uncomfortable sea-level heat, men were cheered in the knowledge that immediate future East African service would be in the much more pleasant climate of 'The Highlands' favoured by European settlers.

Incongruously clad in pristine white shirt and shorts, experienced railway engineers and officials examined, directed, prodded and coaxed the much-travelled dirty old engine until it belched and sprang into life.

All travelling ordered aboard, we were away.

The first wildlife spotted, cameras, many undoubtedly loot from Germany, were soon clicking. Increasingly so as ostriches, gazelle, giraffe and herds of buffalo became prolific. And, to much excitement, at the Athi River, crocodile.

This was something of a Cook's Tour!

At Government expense!

Came something cameras could not adequately capture. A most stunning sunset; but over all too soon! So abruptly terminated, bringing total darkness! With it, the temperature plummetted.

Still wearing daytime tropical kit the sudden chill caught newcomers completely by surprise.

Chugging through a remote but verdant area the suspect engine stuttered to a halt. Shivering, bodies scrambled from carriages to stretch legs and exercise.

From the bush, blanketted natives appeared, watching interestedly.

'Go on! Ask them what time it is!' somebody challenged.

Willing to oblige, those returning from UK leave, not averse to demonstrating expertise with Ki-Swahili, did so. Sans watches, in grinning consultation, those tribesmen astonishingly came up with the correct time to within a couple of minutes!

More and more eyes gleamed through the darkness.

Tribesmen standing at a discreet distance drew nearer, which emboldened others. There we were; sensibly blanketted blacks and foolishly exposed whites thoroughly enjoying the banter.

The Kenya-experienced ought to have known better!

This night exposure was later to spark off serious discussion on the precise incubation period for malaria - struck prostrate as I was much earlier than anyone could believe possible!

It must have been a full hour's delay before the train was again chugging uphill and downhill; and in the light of dawn, following contours, describing large loops. Remarkably from the same seat, all carriages, front and rear in sight, snakelike, forming a complete half circle.

The knowledgeables warned the much interrupted trip would soon be over.

Bits and bobs gathered together, we waited.

Nairobi Station!

What a bustling hive of activity!

And what a nice gesture - a welcoming blast from the band of The King's African Rifles.

Dodging along the crowded platform, the dozen or so destined for Ruiru P & L Depot chased to locate the baggage wallah, each anxious to claim heavy personal baggage last seen going into the hold at Southampton.

There need have been no worry!

All had been off-loaded and placed in line, against a wall, strategically near the exit.

The Baggage man had done his job perfectly!

Precious individual gear was carefully watched as African boys loaded a waiting lorry.

Thanks and appreciations, rightly so, were being showered on our Baggage Wallah. Everything safe and correct. He'd done a marvellous job!

Congratulations ringing in his ears, relieved, satisfied, happy, the Baggage Wallah turned to supervise the humping of the last, his own, valise.

It had been nicked!

Gone!

All having climbed on the lorry, somewhat ungenerously we left him standing there.

Still dementedly screaming:

'Thieving Wogs! Sod bloody Africa!'.

Bwana Fupi's Fire Brigade

During massive demobilisation of African troops, with the first evidence of Mau-Mau activity the juxtaposition of Depot buildings took on important significance.

The long, balconied, timber HQ Discharge Wing housed all departmental offices. The O.C. and the Adjutant each had one of the extreme end rooms.

At the Adjutant's end, just a few yards away stood the Fire Station.

The sprawling Camp, Africa's largest, having many hundreds of huts roofed with rushes, was a fire hazard of alarming proportions. How they had survived something of miracle considering the unlimited supply of cheap cigarettes and matches at the African NAAFI Canteen.

An additional risk existed at the 'chows', the deep hole latrines, these having shafted entrances to a firing point below.

Just as to any boy, fire held a wonderfully strange fascination for the black warrior!

At sunset, tribal chants and dancing to the thumping beat of home-made cowskin drums would regularly be staged around a fire built anywhere between huts.

Which meant a Fire Engine was a must!

This was a three-ton truck, proudly, lovingly, maintained and manned by a permanent African crew.

Prompted by Intelligence, East Africa Command called a secret meeting at its Muthaiga HQ, Nairobi. Counter-measures had been planned for coping with discharged askari expected to run riot in the capital's streets. Having been well trained to maintain discipline, ex-Warrant officers and Sergeants could quite easily incite and manipulate ex-military, of whatever tribe.

Occupying the Adjutant's office, my own small part in the overall plan was to take over the Fire Brigade at the Depot, normally the responsibility of Regimental Police. Put into effect the change had readily been received by the Fire boys as signal recognition of the importance of their fire-fighting status.

In truth, should occasion arise, it would be the Adjutant who would receive the coded alert from Command and get the engine quickly racing into Nairobi to turn hoses on to the rioters.

'Bwana Fupi's Fire Brigade' was born!

Every Bwana had a nickname. 'Fupi' the Swahili equivalent of

'Tich'. One who had lost a finger 'Six Fingers'!

Irrepressibly by nature full of fun himself, it was hardly surprising Bwana Fupi received many false alarms from bored colleagues. Crying wolf too often, the pranks became a nuisance, treated with contempt and the phone slammed down.

Which happened one day when an announcement came through.

'Fire at C Company chow!'

The phone rang again, and a much more urgent voice.

'Seriously, Fire at C Company!'.

Not amused, Fupi snapped a reply.

'Please! Stop messing about, I'm busy!', and again hung up.

The ringing persisted. Eventually answered it proved to be C Company's Commander, Don, a pal.

'Hi! That fire engine. It's definitely wanted!'.

Amongst close friends niceties are superfluous.

'B----off!'

He rang back.

'I must know that engine's on its way!'.

'No! Forget it!'.

Once more the receiver was slammed down.

The ringing persisted.

Removal of the receiver the only escape, that stopped the nonsense!

But not for long.

Crashing through the door, a breathless colleague grabbed and replaced the receiver.

'Colonel's been on! Furious! Insists you answer!'.

An apparently livid Colonel was screaming.

'Cross-my-heart! -There-is-a-bloody-big-fire-at-C-Company-and-you-will-get-the-Engine-out-and-that's-an-official-order!'.

Said with some conviction, maybe it was genuine.

Walking over to the Fire Station, the crew was despatched.

It was too late!

The chow had completely gone up in flames, and drifting sparks taken two large living huts with it!

Well, in the Mess that evening it was good for a laugh! And the end of false alarms for Fupi!

It was the hot season.

Thousands of miles from home, for most all incentive and interest long since gone, intense boredom set in. And all who have been East will know just how depressing that can be!

The usual time-killing late evening card games were drearily in progress; morose, uncommunicative individuals sombrely supping at the bar; others feet up on tables, snoozing. A morbidly quiet, intensely brooding, atmosphere enveloped the Mess.

Being browned off was fairly normal but this extra dejection, this mass boredom was funereal!

Some bods had already called it a day. Soon the Mess would close. There would be the usual steady shuffle quietly towards bunks. Mosquito nets draped, yet another confounded day would be over.

Alone, elbows on bar, a depressed silent Colonel sat staring into his last whisky.

Suddenly, he came alive!

Swinging around he bellowed out.

'Hey! Fupi! What about turning out the Fire Brigade?'.

Drooping, listless characters still around reacted immediately.

'Damn' good idea!'

'This place is like a morgue!'

'Sure would liven things up!'.

'We're game!'.

'Why not?'

The Colonel had the devil in his eyes.

'Right! Everybody out pacey sana! Fupi, alert the Fire Brigade!'.

The emergency call went out.

It was a bright clear night. A full moon - which probably explained everything!

Hastening to the Fire Station, Fupi found agitated members of the crew assembling, boots undone, shirts trailing, pill hats askew, being urged on by the big wide-eyed bush-hatted Sergeant.

'Real fire! Colonel's Hut! Hurry!' instructed Fupi.

Responding to much practised drill the crew clambered aboard. With Bwana seated alongside driver, alarm bell clanging furiously, the lorry roared off into the night.

Hose coupled up, water was very soon cascading down in the vicinity of the Colonel's hut.

'Sergeant, Colonel wants see how good you are night-time Fire call out' advised Fupi, with which the big Sergeant carried the message to each of his men, appealing for more effort, more speed.

For dramatic effect real little fires were gleefully being lit at other spots around; dozens of officers issuing deliberate, conflicting instructions, confusing the Fire Sergeant, bewildering the crew.

'Fire spreading. Run out more hose!' instructed Fupi.

Obligingly, more and yet more hose stretched out in huge convolutions like a writhing monster python! A hopeless spaghetti of tangled hose lay everywhere!

The disturbance had wakened the whole Camp.

To a man, thousands of African troops looked on spellbound, delighted at the big show provided; delighted at the most welcome break to an otherwise monotonous existence.

Swahili-speaking effendis excitedly cavorted about having a wonderful time insistingly reporting fire had spread dangerously. Fire Engine moved one way then another, with boys attempting to lift the hose and falling over, provided hilarious entertainment, all accompanied by an unco-ordinated, bewildering mass of orders.

This was chaos.

The watching African troops, quick to gather what was going on, broadly grinning, contributed in giving advice to the now hapless crew.

All available hose had been put in use; further demands brought crisis never before experienced. The whole affair had become a complete shambles.

Although the Colonel was still enjoying himself, at this high point, to maintain just a modicum of seriousness Bwana Fupi made himself heard.

'Well done Sergeant! Fires out! Stand down!'.

Elated, drinking deep of this glorious opportunity to let the hair down officers crowded around to offer congratulations, together with the wildest, daftest, suggestions on how best to unravel the miles of twisted hose!

At long last, in carnival spirit, a mighty cheer greeted the last roll of hose to be hauled up on to the fire engine!

If the jollifications had then ceased it was later agreed the release valve had worked splendidly.

But the Colonel was not finished!

'All available transport out! he screamed.

Lorries, utilities, Army cars, private cars, motor-bikes, even bicycles, were hauled out, manned and over-manned! Unable to find a seat, officers perched anywhere! Car windows down, legs inside, body out, hands gripping hardtops; anything wild, stupid and different, all joined in.

Led by one Chev, Colonel at the wheel, the bizarre cavalcade moved off. At the rear, fireboys, tired and exhausted, holding on for dear life as the Fire Engine, recklessly driven by Bwana Fupi, struggled to catch up. Headlights flashing, horns blaring, bells clanging, the mad procession careered around the Camp!

At ever increasing speed the Colonel was pursued by the long crocodile in top gear, raising clouds of dust, scattering Africans, enthralled and delighted with the whole caboodle, thrilled at the Colonel and all the Bwanas enjoying themselves.

Around backwaters of the Camp without roads, over bridges intended for foot passage only, the Colonel hair-raisingly zig-zagged on a grand tour, before turning towards that holy of holies, the Depot Parade Ground! Slowing down gave the opportunity for all to catch up. All the time the cacophony of sound increasing. The Fire Engine coming into view was the signal! With stacatto hootings, the intention was clear!

Round and round the Parade Ground! Three whole laps! Trapping hundreds and hundreds of half-dressed boys! Then, startlingly, the Chev veered and made for the middle, carving its way through the multitude! Impossible! Pandemonium!

Everything ground to a stop. One last long blast from all horns, headlights flashing, and a loud continuous clang from the fire engine brought to an end a grotesque performance which could never possibly be repeated! It was all over!

In high spirits, askaris returned to their huts.

In jubilation, effendis piled in to the deserted Mess. Every possible light switched on, the bar was plundered. Yes, ruled the Colonel, all drinks would be 'on the house'.

Boredom and gloom had truly been banished!

Gradually the celebrations subsided. In the small hours exhausted but very happy officers settled down to grab some sleep.

Always a light sleeper, I needn't have bothered!

Stirring within the hour, a distant faint rumbling couldn't be placed. Listening intently it was not dissimilar to tribal chanting. It couldn't be that of course. Not in the middle of the night. But it sounded like many distant voices - certainly something coming from some part of the vast Camp. Curiosity aroused, I would slip out of bed and listen at the window.

Wow! Perhaps two miles away a red glow lit up the sky! Fire! Real fire!

Pulling jacket and trousers over pyjamas, and chasing outside towards the Fire Station, it was no surprise to bump headlong into a messenger sent from the Guard Room.

'Cap'n! Cap'n! Big fire! B Company. Message gone Fire Station!' he gasped.

'Bells! Run! Run! Tell them NO BELLS!'

'Dio effendi!' and he sped off.

By the time the Engine arrived B Company's large stores building was going up fast! This was the largest Store, in which all greatcoats were deposited – greatcoats taken from outgoing Africans immediately prior to their leaving in large drafts on safari, homeward bound! Those boys resented the substitute issue of one blanket! They felt cheated! Felt all symbolism of their service stripped from them! The choice of building was clear!

And this was the peculiar humour of the African. Those Bwanas could have their fun playing at fires! We'll give them the real thing!

Accompanied by the African Duty Warrant Officer an appalled young Colonial Orderly Officer had reached the scene from the Guard Room. He was clearly nervous with hundreds of blacks excitedly pressing around. (It was common knowledge a fearful officer had taken fright, and fled, some time back!)

Pleased to see another white face he was surprised to be told to grin, relax, and treat the whole affair as a joke; also quite unnecessary to alert either the Colonel or the Company Commander.

The African Sergeant Major quickly did his stuff.

Anyone tapping a drum would have it confiscated.

Everyone would immediately return to huts and there would be a full inspection within fifteen minutes. It worked!

Overtired fireboys did what they could.

Back in the European quarters, the Officers Mess, the Sergeants Mess, slept on.

Three hours later, heading to snatch a few winks before Reveille, it was necessary for Fupi to pass the Colonel's hut.

A window flew open.

'What's all the smoke Fupi? What's happened?'

'Boys been excited Sir! Nothing to worry about!'

The Colonel went back to his bed.

The morning parade had been specially planned.

Never before had all Companies, Pioneers, together with East African Military Labour Service units, POW's, plus multi-national admin staff, all assembled together. 'Impossible, but let's try it' had been the wheeze concocted during the night's revelry.

Thousands poured in and around the Parade Ground.

Over the impressive Guard Room the flag was flying.

Occupying a place of honour on the Parade Ground, facing the Guard Room, stood the Fire Brigade, the big Sergeant, proudest of all, right marker.

Every conceivable ceremonial, all possible bull, would be enacted to make this Parade most special.

From somewhere, someone had found an old fashioned hand megaphone, using which the Colonel addressed the vast parade as best he could. Thousands wouldn't have heard a word. He thanked all present for their service and loyalty: wished them all the best luck when they returned to their own villages, wives and families.

Then came the raison-d'être for the big get-together.

Solemnly striding from the balconied Guard Room, flanked by Second-in-Command and other staff, the Colonel inspected the night's heroes.

He then advised the whole Parade of a presentation to each member of the Fire Brigade.

Led by their Sergeant, each mounted the balcony for a handshake and a special award – a large parcel of goodies from the NAAFI!

Three cheers called for by the Colonel produced a succession of roars befitting a Wembley crowd witnessing the collection of the FA Cup!

The occasion would be long remembered.

And of course this over-spill from the night's merriment had combined to do the trick!

Killed boredom! Stone dead!

Thereafter, people were actually cheerful! Smiling at each other! White and Black!

The night's hilarity was timely.

Incidentally, the demob procedure of sending out large drafts all over East Africa, from Northern Territories down to the Cape, with the issue of Last Pay Certificates redeemable only by personal attendance on the District Commissioner nearest each man's home 'boma' was successful beyond the wildest dreams.

The system effectively prevented massive crowds of ex-askari settling in Nairobi!

The expected disorderly rioting didn't happen! Which was most fortunate!

But Bwana Fupi's real role with the Fire Brigade remained an untold, very closely kept, secret!

Until now!

Gunner

From the North-East of England, since initially reporting to R.A. Woolwich, he had travelled far and wide. Posted to many places with unpronounceable names. Through desert and jungle.

One of the Forgotten Army.

He'd put in some service!

Months had become years, yet always UK leave had eluded him!

Finally, he'd landed up in Kenya, not far from Nairobi.

VE Day, and much more importantly to him, VJ Day, had come and gone.

The War over, Geordie was angry he wouldn't be going home immediately, but would be privileged to have fourteen days 'local leave' down on the coast near Mombasa. Some place called Malindi or something. He couldn't remember: wasn't all that interested.

After joining up his first Leave from Red Barracks had been Embarkation Leave when he'd married the sweetheart of his schooldays. Both seventeen. The ceremony, an austere affair, had been in keeping with the times – ration books, blackout and all that.

Little enough to pay the parson, honeymooning was impossible. A handful of relatives met for a few drinks at the girl's home, where Gunner and his young wife stayed for the rest of the Leave.

No chance of setting up a home of their own of course. There wouldn't be much point with the future so uncertain. Besides which the Council house waiting list was frighteningly long. He'd stuck his name down at the Town Hall, only on the insistence of his old man.

In the back streets of Nairobi, near the Stanley Hotel, he was now sitting brooding in Auntie's Pantry – one of those welcoming places cheerfully set up by Colonial ladies desperately keen to do something for the boys sent out from the Old Country.

Over almost free tea and buns Geordie cursed his luck to a fellow Gunner who was based near the Airport; venting his feelings specifically on the dam' silly LILOP Scheme and the injustice of it all.

'Hell! Three whole years without Home Leave! Bloody criminal! What's the good of hanging around on some hot African beach? I flippin' well ought to have got UK Leave!'

'Tell you what' came the response 'I know this bloke in the USAF.

Yanks are always boasting about taking quick flips over to London and back'.

'Alright for them!' said Geordie 'No chance of getting in on that racket! Home and back in a fortnight! Some hope!'

'Oh well, you never know! Anyhow, I'll mention it to him. What're the dates?'

Geordie was surprised his mate had taken this so seriously, but the dates of the local leave had been scribbled down on an old cigarette packet.

The two went their ways, Geordie not giving any thought to the scatterbrain idea.

Not so his pal.

The Yanks, impishly delighting in defying the rules, were quite co-operative, though they couldn't even start to guess on the prospect of how ETD's and ETA's would work out. Yeah! Sure! Been done often enough! The English guy would just have to chance his luck!

Meeting up again in Auntie's Pantry, Gunner heard all this. It was something he thought impossible. But how really wonderful it would be if it came off!

Dare he chance it? The leave was booked. God knows when the next lot would be, and his pal seemed quite sure it could be done! Pondering hard, perhaps after all it would be worth taking the risk? The more he thought about it the more his mind focused on this one and only opportunity of beating that daft LILOP scheme. Yes, he'd give it a go!

The Leave date arrived. Fourteen days Pass safely pocketted, he made straight for the Airport area.

If the whole thing fizzled out: if he couldn't get airborne, well, mooching around in Nairobi wouldn't be all that bad!

Finding his pal, it was easy to stay incognito in the same RA quarters to await a call from the American. It came almost immediately!

He was stowed away in a U.S. plane, destination 'England' – that's all they could tell him.

Well, wherever it landed, however far from Newcastle, hitch-hiking any distance wouldn't be a problem.

Put in with a young GI doing the same unauthorised trip a note was passed giving a London telephone number for picking up gen on what would be the more awkward return arrangements.

The dream became fact.

His young wife, parents, in-laws and relatives were surprised, delighted, and most impressed with the initiative he'd shown! Fancy pulling off such a totally unexpected visit home from so far away! Oh the marvels of air travel!

Despite hiccups which threatened to wreck very complicated return arrangements, most particularly during the devious plot to circumvent security guard checks, Gunner did actually manage to arrive back at Nairobi Airport in time to rejoin his Unit.

Yanks had sworn him to secrecy. That secrecy would be honoured! Didn't breathe a word to anyone in his own outfit!

Now he was quite content to sweat out the long and dreary wait until his Demob Release Group number came up!

Months passed.

Men with much longer service, and who had been Overseas without home leave longer than Gunner were first to go. Lucky them! Down to Mombasa and off by troopship away from this 'bado kidogo' land! Gunner realised he was that much younger: would have to be patient. His turn would come – eventually.

Never having been much of a writer, letters home became even more rare and still more brief; mostly about the magic unknown date when his army days would be over.

Out of the blue, unexpectedly summoned to attend Battery Office HQ, Gunner listened to the Battery Commander's cautious enquiry.

'Have you implicit faith in your wife, Gunner?'

'Of course, Yes Sir!' stammered a surprised Geordie.

'Supposing she let you down, broke her trust, would you stand by her?'

'Trust, Sir? How d'you mean Sir?'

'Well me lad, War Office have checked. You have been Overseas more than three years. You agree?'

'Yes Sir'.

'Did you know your wife has claimed child allowance?'

'She hasn't told me Sir'.

Unprepared as he was, Gunner blurted out his secret air trip! He'd beaten the LILOP scheme!

The babe was his alright.

Unfortunately, when Gunner's Demob release date finally *did* come up he was left behind to languish in Nairobi.

Detained at His Majesty's pleasure!

Chameleon

Colonials, as you would expect, were natural leaders of the black African at war.

A number had been in the safari Big Game business. Had met the nobility, privileged and wealthy from all parts of the world. Had made romantic attachments with offspring of royalty. Could enthral with stories of many a resplendent safari between the Wars.

Nick had been the undoubted star of all white hunters.

When our own young and popular heir to the throne (he who later abdicated) visited East Africa it was always Nick who organised things, took command of the entourage, becoming almost a personal friend.

His close rapport with all tribes, his wide knowledge of the bush and wildlife, his immense comprehension of weaponry and uncanny accuracy as a shot, had built up for him popular international acclaim and respect.

Quiet, soft-spoken, he rarely indulged in conversation with those around at the Depot to which he had returned. New arrivals, knowing nothing of him, had noted this, taking him for what he was: courteous, modest, and undoubtedly experienced. More than a gentleman – a man's man. No ordinary Captain.

We were talking of chameleons. From his room he had brought and presented me with one of his pet favourites.

'Your boy won't spend overmuch time in your room with this around!' he murmured.

He was of course right. The boy nervously regarded it as possessing some evil.

In those early days – early to we who had arrived via Germany – a Depot vacancy had arisen for which Nick would surely be the obvious choice. He was not given the appointment because it carried the rank of Major. 'Why?' we had queried. We were duly enlightened!

Apparently his home was somewhere near Nairobi. Unexpectedly early, he had been returned from the Middle East. As a surprise, unannounced, he made for home, to find a British officer in bed with his wife. Strolling to his gun room, he had selected one of his cherished rifles and blasted at the intruder. In the private parts!

He had not been dismissed the Service. That would hardly have been punishment.

The Law people and the Judge Advocate General's Department, having no precedent on which to work, continued to procrastinate.

Meantime the Court of Inquiry, followed by Court Martial, had ruled on one aspect. Rank would be reduced to Captain – permanently.

Which explained why such an obviously outstanding and talented character hadn't been made up to be my Major and O.C. at Discharge Wing.

Within days he was posted away. Up to Jinja, and nothing more was heard of him.

The chameleon was well looked after, properly fed as instructed, and became a loveable, lively room companion, providing endless pleasure, and of course a constant reminder of the white hunter whose military and marital life had become such a shambles.

At Nairobi's 87 General Military Hospital, it was puzzling to find in there an escort of two officers seated flanking the bed of one patient who had been through extensive, complicated, surgery. Fitted up with a Heath Robinson contraption of tubes, he had become mentally unbalanced and on a number of occasions had attempted suicide. Like some wild animal, had to be carefully watched – hence the all-round-the-clock permanent guard.

Slowly going insane, this was the white hunter's victim!

Having gone to the hospital for consultation but held for prompt operation I had taken the early precaution of telephoning the Depot seeking protection of personal kit and chattels, and of course the chameleon.

Manyana rampant, nothing had been done.

It came as no surprise to learn my boy, taking his Last Pay Certificate, had gone on an outgoing draft, leaving my room in disarray, and on the broad windowsill ravaged remains of the chameleon. Rather than let it free, a machete had seen its end.

Months later, with demob well overdue, and on my feet, though in extremis, thanks to the connivance of a friendly M.O. a place on a home-going troopship had been secured. Prior to meeting the assembly at Nairobi Station a digression to the Depot sixteen miles out would be necessary to gather together and arrange onward transmission of personal belongings.

The final influx of askari from the Middle East were now discharged and scattered all over East Africa.

The place was deserted. In the last rites of closing down for good.

Right from the commencement of seeing service here two or three of the outermost end rooms of the long timber hutted sleeping quarters had been abandoned – left to the white ants, which, thickly cushioned, had plastered all walls. Such invasion was a remorseless process, quite incapable of prevention.

I wondered if they had taken my room over.

Dragging myself along the corridor towards my door, this had been roughly boarded across in a belated gesture of security. The adjoining room sure had been taken over by the ants!

Door freed and pushed open, remarkably those ants had given me a miss, which was some consolation.

In shocking chaos, possibly half my possessions remained: which was almost pleasing. Less to pack!

Like the room itself I was a bit of a wreck.

The breathtaking beautiful Africa was not for me: it was for the fit and the strong. This ritual of sorting out disordered remnants, an effort, would be the end of a chapter.

Seated, resting, surveying the jumbled mess, the badly chipped window shelf confirmed a machete really had been used in savage frenzy.

That exquisitely created harmless creature, which had brought such joy, belonged to Africa – could so easily have survived here. Didn't deserve the cruel end inflicted by a berserk servant boy!

How lucky for him Nick the white hunter had not been the last to quit the Depot – which he could well have been!

Radar – Top Secret

He was in the Senior Service.

Had been involved with a motor boat flotilla.

Knew all there was to know about installations at Kilindini Harbour, Mombasa.

Knew the ropes: particularly anything to do with troopships.

For demob we were to be passengers back to the U.K. together.

I came to know him very well.

This matelot had given service, man and boy, for over thirty years. He was saying goodbye to the Royal Navy, the only life he'd known, and would pick up a sizeable pension.

As we were scheduled to share cabin accommodation there was every reason to believe this would be very much up to standard. Of course it was much more than that!

But there was no question about it. All those years travelling the world had done something to him. He was quite mad!

Meeting up as we approached the ship's gangway he pointed to a large crate standing with others waiting to be shipped aboard.

'That's mine!' he chirruped triumphantly.

Boldly labelled 'Radar – Top Secret' the crate was addressed to a high ranking officer at some UK Naval Command. A more than familiar name. In fact a household name known to everybody. It had the many markings of an important official consignment.

'All correctly documented! Full of booze!' he confided.

Troopships of course are always 'dry'.

'Surely', I chided 'You can't gamble with King's Regulations, and your good record?'

I was confident of the KR's but not the other.

'Squared the boys! All organised!' he said, most emphatically.

From an upper deck we watched the buzz of quayside activity and the late loadings.

Suddenly the matelot cursed.

Half a dozen black boys were struggling up the gangway with his crate. The Purser stood at the top, pointing, directing them the way to the hold.

'He'll have 'em lost going that way!' our seadog choked.

Off he sprinted.

We watched him push his way through a crowded lower deck. Spotted him chasing after the boys: remonstrating with them, persuading them, steering them acrobatically up a companion way. Crew members were protesting, dismissively barging the boys back.

Our madman got his way.

The crate reposed in a small storage room adjoining the cabin suite, and, incredibly, he'd somehow acquired a key!

Here was this naval lunatic blatantly cocking a snoot at authority! Seven cabin mates had no choice! Like it or not, they were let into the secret.

Once at sea, a procedure evolved.

Drinks available three times each day.

A Goan steward, bribed to bring ice cubes, and punctually, never missed mention of the risk involved.

'If Cap'n find out he play blubberly me!'

His counter-bribe successful more than once!

Need I mention that the Cabin-suite, one of the most luxurious, was on the 'starboard home' side and adequately spacious even accommodating eight officers?

Initially each occupant could invite two guests at any one time to drink their fill.

Reaching the Red Sea, the sessions doubled and trebled, and in a grand gesture the limitation of guests cancelled.

These surreptitious convivial gatherings very much punctuated the day and dangerously enlivened the evenings.

More and more made privy to the set up, quite naturally each staked a claim to regular attendance without fear of being rebuffed! Officers of all Services, all ranks, drawn into the web woven by our conspirator! He reckoned they couldn't all be Court-martialled!

We, his cabin companions, hopelessly, inextricably, compromised; at the very heart of the calumny! We, who had always 'put the men first' denied of such proud claim. Thoroughly trapped!

Days got hotter. The attraction of iced drink, irresistible. Chatting time perforce reduced, individuals were unceremoniously pushed out to make room for others – naval types, Colonels, Squadron Leaders, jockeying for footspace.

But attending rank was not good enough for our wild man!

'Brigadier on board! Bring on the Brigadier!' he shrieked.

Stock in the crate still plentiful, spurred on by the vast secret scandal of his creation, now having almost a hundred accomplices, the increase in rank at each session had been accidental, but now he was demanding someone of still higher rank!

Maniac! Almost as if he was deliberately tempting disaster!

To howls of laughter a mock Court of Inquiry was underway, though it became more on the lines of a Conquistadorial Imposition!

He suspected of being the most senior present must be charged – on pain of being thrown overboard – with the privilege of inviting the Brigadier, highest rank travelling!

The guilty, determined by noisiest acclamation, immediately sallied forth; to the Star Chamber's amazement returning minutes later accompanied by one Brigadier delightedly expressing amusement and appreciation!

So, before reaching Port Said, every commissioned rank travelling, bar none, had figured amongst habitués of that drinking den!

Albeit a troopship, as on peacetime cruises, it was a privilege to receive an invitation to sit at the Captain's table. This, at no time, had come my way. Why should it?

Within hours of land, the honour came. Which surprised me.

Still more surprising was to hear the lunatic Naval character proudly announcing he'd been gifted with a similar invitation. To the same meal!

With the utmost courtesy the Captain insisted I should sit beside him. Embarrassed, flattered, puzzled, I did just that; to discover the mad matelot had been equally placed!

Formalities, introductions, and the niceties of welcome over, dinner was in full swing.

Choosing the right moment, the Captain motioned to within confidential whispering distance the two seated at his immediate port and starboard side.

'Philistines and Hypocrites!' he breathed 'A whole shipful! Think I'll change course! Dump the bloody lot of you in Australia!'

His eyes had the smile of a man who, in his time, had seen everything!

Man in the Next Bed

Switched from the squalor and activity of Germany to the sunshine and lack of urgency of Kenya, even the halt and lame benefitted.

The Depot XI brought together was a team of 'has beens', now of low medical category, excused all parades and marching, mostly engaged on admin, cooking, batman or quartermastering duties. All had at one time played in good class soccer. Old heads on 'old' bodies deliberately slowed the game down to suit the heat and altitude, strolling through matches with minimum effort to such good effect all opposition had been swept aside.

A challenge was received.

A selected side representative of the whole of East Africa Command would meet the Depot XI.

The venue, Nairobi Stadium: which some years later was to be renamed Kenyatta Stadium.

It would be a grand affair, and, just like the big matches way back home, with a band. The King's African Rifles! Admission free would ensure a gate of many thousands – those black Africans football mad!

At the last minute, an upset. One player unavailable! For this special occasion, this showpiece, pressed to make a comeback, the temptation was too great! What a crazy, GHASTLY mistake! Ground like concrete, sixteen stones of goalkeeper crashed into fragile limbs. The RAMC boys did a good stretcher job, the usual magic sponge having failed, miserably.

For a month, an orange-sized lump travelled round previously-damaged spine and buttocks. Fourteen weeks in hospital followed yet another operation.

A number of patients were casualties from Germany, shipped out purely for recuperation. The Kenya climate would aid recovery.

The man in the next bed was one.

We had earlier become acquainted in those Cafe-Clubs which the dear ladies of Nairobi established for Service people.

Excused duties, he just pottered about, making himself useful wherever, and whenever, he felt like it.

His was a sad case.

Quite probably his story never has been told.

He had been though Hell!

Like many more, his tortured body would for ever be a constant reminder of Service days. I have often wondered how he survived. If he did.

For a long time Ken had been familiar with hospitals. Operation after operation. But a more cheerful bloke you wouldn't meet anywhere!

His Regiment? The Warwickshires.

His Release Group coincided with my own. The authorities hoped to patch him up sufficiently to meet Demob date: which was wishful thinking.

Somewhere with the BLA, in close combat, his platoon had been cut off; trapped in an exposed house. Orders were to hold the position. Hopelessly outnumbered, men fell all round him, dying the most agonising deaths. For four days they held out. Shelled, machine-gunned, none expected to live. Few did.

It took as many as three Companies to regain lost ground and reach him, for which rescue his Major was awarded the MC.

The man in the next bed had not been given any award. No recognition whatsoever. Not even a mention in despatches!

What he did get was more pieces of shrapnel in his body and head than there are days in the year!

Laughingly, he marvelled at being alive. We marvelled with him!

Nights in that hospital were the worst.

During daylight things were different. Helping nurses with the dirtiest of tasks, the Italian POW ward orderlies, always in good humour, attending to dressings cases in turn, would screen each bed. Yells of pain would be drowned by laughing encouragement from all round! Brutal, jesting suggestions advising the Italians how best to inflict still further torture!

And things were happening to occupy the mind!

The walking wounded up to all sorts of tricks, keeping everybody amused and occupied; hurrying nurses, professionally tolerant, the target for endless good-natured banter; colleagues visiting from a variety of Units bringing in news of the outside world. Yes, the day brought much distraction.

But the night!!

Pills and potions dispensed, vast mosquito nets anchored to the ceiling would be released, draping each bed.

Lights out, figures moved phantom-like.

The lucky slept.

The afflicted snatched sleep only in exhaustion.

When not silently flitting about, the red and white of a nurse's uniform would be seen reflected from a shaded light at the end of the

Ward. One of those never-to-be-forgotten, much loved QUAIMNS, palefaced, seemingly always studying between ministrations of the long night watch.

In the normality of groans and sharp stifled reactions to pain, somebody, in a release of tension and agony would wildly shriek out. Men, voices hushed, would discuss and anxiously identify from which cocooned bed the scream had come – far from being disturbed, grateful for the opportunity of communication.

Those nights were cruel. God! So cruel!

The mosquito net, like a mist covering each man's lonely island, shrouded individual thought and struggle. Anguished minds in competition with disturbed bodies! Messages frequently came from those lonely islands with the same alarming suddenness. Urgent, garbled cries of warning exploding from men subconsciously re-living things past.

Particularly from the man in the next bed.

Fighting against the odds.

Though I could not see him I could not help but be aware of his perpetual tossing about, seeking some posture which might provide easement. A hopeless quest!

Dawn was eagerly awaited. Always welcomed.

Ken would be the first with a cheery 'Good Morning fellers!' almost as if he had slumbered blissfully, like a child, all night.

In the flush of action and excitement in the field of *course* brave deeds merited honoured decoration.

In my book of continuing glory, Ken's *post-war* bravery carries more medals than have ever been minted.

I think of a talented cousin. My best man. School chums. All killed in action or lost at sea.

I think of a life-time's pal, a Manxman and also once a Sapper, who entered into the darkness of total mental silence.

But it's when I think of that man in the next bed I realize why it is those in The Legion or BLESMA, or any Old Comrades Association have kept the faith: have brought evening sunshine and cheer in succouring the needs of any Ex-Service man, who, sooner rather than later, will answer the final call.

No hero!

'Just another' Number, Rank and Name.